The Reckless Gun

Yuma Prison holds the most notorious prisoners in the West, and Dutch Henry Vandyke is one of them. Sentenced to twenty years' hard labour for his crimes, Dutch was never meant to see the outside world again, and for that he had Sheriff Chad Gleeson to thank.

But now Vandyke is out, and has sworn to get even with the man who put him there. Sheriff Gleeson must now face his most formidable foe and summon all his strength if he is to survive a shot from the Reckless Gun.

The Reckless Gun

Dale Graham

A Black Horse Western

ROBERT HALE · LONDON

ISBN 978-0-7198-1303-0

Robert Hale Limited
Clerkenwell House
Clerkenwell Green
London EC1R 0HT

www.halebooks.com

Typeset by
Derek Doyle & Associates, Shaw Heath
Printed and bound in Great Britain by
CPI Antony Rowe, Chippenham and Eastbourne

ONE

FROM FLAGSTAFF . . .

The stagecoach jounced and rattled its way across the bleak tableland comprising northern Arizona's Mogollon Plateau. Its next destination was the booming settlement of Casa Grande which lay a good five days' ride to the south.

Garishly painted in bright red with fancy gold markings, the coach offered a welcome splash of colour amidst the jaded, flat tones of the dominant sagebrush terrain. A cloud of ochre dust was churned up in its wake as the driver expertly held the team of six to a steady canter.

They needed to reach the relay station at Sedona by nightfall. Too soon and the passengers would be forced to hang about for their supper. That could lead to complaints. But too late and all the vittles would have been eaten. Bull Ferris was a veteran of this route. He knew every twist and turn of the lonely trail, the name of every prominent rock and mountain peak.

He pointed out a soaring monolith coming up on the right side of the trail.

'That there is Cochise Butte,' he opined to his buddy Three-Fingered Jimmy Dean, who was riding shotgun. 'They say its shape is the spitting image of the Apache renegade. Can't say I've ever gotten close enough to find out.'

'Don't look nothing like him,' huffed Dean with a muted croak. 'I know 'cause the bastard attacked our patrol in the Gila Valley when I was riding with the 6th Cavalry under Colonel Crook. I was one of the few to come out of that fracas with a whole skin.' He jabbed a finger at his left hand. 'Excepting for this, which was caused by a buck's scalping knife. He was after taking all five to hang round his belt. But my pistol took care of the critter afore he could finish the job.'

Dean had been invalided out of the army following his recovery. That had been ten years before. Since then he had been riding shotgun for the Overland.

'It looks to me more like Geronimo,' interjected Raccoon Adler, who was one of the passengers riding on the roof.

His partner, Curly Dick, grunted. 'If'n you ask me, all those red devils look alike.'

Thereafter, they lapsed into silence. For once old Bull was lost for words.

Four hours had passed since the Concord had set off on this initial leg of the journey. But this particular trip was not one of the regular weekly runs operated by the Butterfield Stagecoach Company. It was an extra which had been laid on to transport a particularly valuable cargo of gold bullion.

As a consequence, the coach had been accorded its own escort of four mounted troopers commanded by an officer. At Sedona, a new patrol would take over, escorting the coach as far as Casa Grande. The final stage was then across country to the territorial bank vault at Globe.

The bluecoats rode two on either side of the coach with Lieutenant Calvin Saunders taking up a forward position. The aim was to deter the felonious attentions of any road agents who might be operating in the area. Saunders was a junior officer and this was only his second command in the field. He sat proudly in the saddle, back straight, eyes surveying the terrain ahead.

Any bandits foolish enough to try robbing this particular stagecoach would be summarily dealt with. Nonetheless, the lonely terrain made the lieutenant nervous. As a consequence he would be more than glad to hand over responsibility for the bullion to another patrol once they reached the trading post at Sedona.

Due to its unusual entry on to the schedule, the coach carried only six passengers instead of the usual full complement of fifteen; that would include six inside with a further nine crammed up on top.

The best seats were amply padded behind the front boot facing backwards. Yet even with the coach supported between oxhide strips acting as shock absorbers, it was still a very bumpy ride. Four passengers willing to pay the extra charge rode inside, with the other two up top. Raccoon Adler and Curly Dick Tranter had settled themselves down between the luggage.

So far little conversation had been forthcoming between the inside passengers. If truth be told, it was too durned hot for meaningless tittle-tattle.

A tall, good-looking man, clean-shaven and well dressed, extracted a silk bandanna and wiped the sweat from his brow. The sun had climbed to its highest point in the cloudless azure sky. The other man beside him was dozing, his hat pulled down to hide his face.

'Shouldn't be too long now before we reach Sedona,' the man said, addressing a young woman. 'Are you travelling far, miss?'

'I am taking up an appointment in Casa Grande as the schoolteacher,' she replied, breathing heavily while fanning her delicate complexion with a lace handkerchief. 'I never realized how hot it can become out here.'

The man next to her belched loudly, then immediately pushed his half-empty bottle of whiskey under her nose. 'Care for a snort, ma'am?' he burbled.

The offer was politely declined with an imperious sniff.

Hyram Gandy shrugged and took a heavy swig himself, one of many he had already imbibed during this leg of the journey. He then decided to add his bit to the burgeoning conflab.

'I'm in bones, miss,' he blurted out, jabbing a finger at the roof. 'My goods are sitting up yonder.'

The girl swallowed nervously. 'Y-you m-mean, sir, that you are an undertaker?' she stammered, clearly assuming that a dead body was also on the passenger list.

The little man emitted a raucous guffaw at the suggestion. 'No, lady, you've gotten it all wrong,' he said, shaking with mirth. 'The bones are my samples.' He paused, offering the girl a leery wink. Another belch followed. 'I travel in fertilizers. Sell 'em to the sodbusters. Bones grind down into good feed for the crops.'

Gandy took another swig from his rapidly declining source of liquor. Swaying drunkenly, he lurched into the lady, much to her further distaste.

The tall man leaned across and grabbed the bottle, throwing it out the window.

'Hey, Mr,' complained Gandy. His ruddy features were blotchy, eyes blurred. 'What you done that for?'

'You're annoying the lady, fella,' rapped the Good Samaritan. 'And it seems to me like you've had more than enough hooch for this trip.'

Lucy Calendar smiled her thanks to the handsome stranger. He bobbed his smart grey Stetson in acknowledgement, revealing a shock of long blond hair. She noticed that the man had a slight intonation in his voice that she couldn't quite place. He certainly wasn't from around these parts. A natural decorum prevented her from enquiring further.

Hungry eyes silently devoured the innocent creature sitting opposite. This hombre was more used to the avaricious pawing of saloon queens. The girl opposite was a new experience for him, and one to be savoured at leisure. He had never come into contact with a schoolma'am before.

The girl completely failed to heed her admirer's lustful ogling. 'Do you think we are in danger of being attacked, sir?' she asked, indicating the presence of the troopers. 'I have been warned that Dutch Henry Vandyke and his gang have been terrorizing this part of the territory.'

The man shook his head. 'I don't think a comely girl like you will have any need to fear Dutch Henry, miss,' the man reassured her. 'These soldier boys are here to protect us as well as the cargo being carried.'

'It's gold bullion, you know,' slurred Gandy, jabbing a finger at the tall man. 'There must be a lot of the yellow stuff for them to send an armed escort of troopers.'

The man ignored the comment. He had eyes only for the girl. He leaned across, holding out his hand. 'My name is John Smith, by the way. I'd like to introduce my colleague here, Mr Jess Beaman.' He nudged the sleeping form in the ribs. All he received back was a turgid grunt. 'But as you see, he ain't as polite as me. And who might you be, miss?'

She shook the proffered appendage. Smith held the tiny hand for somewhat longer than acceptable propriety allowed for.

'Miss Lucy Calendar, late of Kansas City,' was the diffident response as she tugged her hand free.

'Mind if'n I call you Luce?' asked the smirking admirer, the forced sense of decorum momentarily slipping.

'I most certainly do mind, Mr Smith,' snapped the girl, turning her attention to a herd of deer that were running parallel with the coach. This man was becoming rather too familiar for her taste.

The galloping herd appeared to be keeping pace with them some fifty yards distant.

'Looks like we have ourselves a race here,' observed Adler to his buddy up on the roof. Curly Dick grinned.

The two mountain men enjoyed nothing better than wagering against each other, anything and everything that took their fancy. They each placed bets as to which animal would win before the coach reached the next butte up ahead.

The running pack had also been noticed by the troopers, who had been sneering insolently at their greenhorn officer's back. Private Abe Wenger sensed that there was fun to be had here.

Before anything more could be said by the passengers inside the coach or their more hardy companions up top, the sharp report of a rifle broke into the tense moment. One of the troopers had withdrawn his breech-loading Springfield and quickly snapped off a shot. A wild hallooing broke out as the last animal in the pack fell to the ground. The rest of the herd quickly dispersed in panic.

The coach rumbled to a halt as the officer came back to admonish the culprit and enquire as to the cause of the unwarranted disturbance.

'What is going on here?' Lieutenant Saunders snapped in his finest West Point accent. 'Who gave you permission to loose off that shot, Private Wenger?'

'I was only thinking of tonight's supper, sir,' wheedled the accused trooper, trying to conceal a smirk.

11

'Doesn't the lieutenant think that deer meat will make for a much tastier meal than fried beans and fatback?' A murmuring of accord from the other troopers greeted this eminently sensible logic.

But the officer's authority had been challenged. He needed to reassert himself.

'You had no right firing off that rifle without my permission,' he snorted, squaring his narrow shoulders.

'But Wenger is right, sir,' said one of the soldier's comrades in support. 'We don't get much chance for a good meal while on patrol. This was an opportunity too good to miss. Wouldn't you say so, sir?'

Saunders hesitated. This was not the officers' mess. All military personnel out on patrol without exception were forced by circumstances to eat the same unwholesome grub. Deer meat was indeed a delicacy rarely encountered in the field.

The others sensed their superior's vacillation. They vigorously nodded their heads, including the coach driver.

But it was another obliging remark that swayed Saunders in favour of the unexpected action.

'Don't you reckon he was being resourceful, sir?' Private Jagger enunciated with a firm assurance. 'After all, that's what the colonel is always encouraging us to do, isn't it? "Try to use your initiative at all times, men," is what he's always telling us.'

The officer did not need any further encouragement in acceding to this unexpected development.

'You are right, Jagger,' he declared firmly as if it was his own decision. 'Sling the carcase up on the coach roof. We'll have it skinned and prepared for supper when we reach Sedona.'

But the young lieutenant still needed to save face and not appear weak in front of his men. His next remark was rasping and bluntly delivered. 'But in future, Private Wenger, if you feel an overwhelming urge to . . . use your initiative, make sure you seek my consent first.'

'Yes, sir,' came back the equally forthright reply, which was accompanied by a smart, parade-ground salute.

The shot had awakened the slumbering form of Jess Beaman. He leaned out of the window. 'Any chance of us sharing that meat, soldier boy?' he enquired hopefully, rubbing the grit from his eyes.

'Afraid not, Mr,' said the resourceful perpetrator of the tasty acquisition. 'It's just a young calf. So there's only enough for us military guys. And seeing as we're doing all the work in keeping you folks safe, this can be our bonus.'

'I'm sure there will be more than sufficient to go round,' interjected the lieutenant, eager to regain the upper hand. 'Private Wenger has been rather overdoing the buffalo steaks of late, judging by his spreading gut.'

Saunders chuckled uproariously at his witty riposte.

Apart from a scowling Wenger, the other troopers joined in the spirited laughter as they resumed their places on either side of the coach.

Moments later the driver cracked his whip, urging the team back into motion.

Smith tried to cajole the attractive passenger opposite into further conversation. But Miss Calendar was
only prepared to respond in cool, monosyllabic utter-
ances. As a result Smith's amorous intentions stumbled
to an undignified halt.

The rest of the journey was made in silence.

Jess Beaman concealed a sly smirk as he threw a dis-
paraging glare towards his partner. He made certain,
however, that the other man did not witness his con-
demnation. Smith was darned touchy when it came to
his predilection for the opposite sex. The trouble was,
it had gotten them into some nasty scrapes over the
years. The guy reckoned he was the good Lord's gift to
women.

Although Beaman had to concede that his partner
possessed the looks and charm that made the inviting
task all the easier.

It was always the same when a pretty face smiled at
him. His normal penchant was for the ones who had
standing in the community, usually by being married to
an important official. Smith could not resist such
women. He especially revelled in thumbing his nose at
puffed-up grandees.

There was that time when they were resting up in
Cimarron over in New Mexico territory. The mayor of
the town had taken umbrage to him and the boys hallooing up and down the street, firing off their pistols.
He had ordered the marshal to curtail their raucous
pleasuring.

As a result Smith was fined twenty dollars.

Simmering with resentment against the pompous

official, he determined to teach the guy a lesson.

Mayor Heffridge had a particularly alluring wife. What was such a delectable creature doing with this bumped-up toad? Smith made it his business to meet up with the woman while her husband was otherwise engaged on council business out of town. His magnetic charisma had easily won the dame over.

That same night, Smith had claimed to be having a loose horseshoe fixed by the blacksmith. He would not be joining the rest of the boys in the saloon until later. The next thing Beaman knew was a noisy outcry of indignation outside in the street. It was followed by gunfire.

Dashing outside, he was stunned to see his buddy stumbling across the street literally with his pants down. A man was leaning out of a window in the hotel opposite. It was the mayor, and he was hollering at the fleeing lothario. Clearly the guy had returned home earlier than expected and caught the offending pair in a compromising situation.

'Come back here, you lecherous rat!' he yelled, shaking a fist at the fleeing seducer while fending off his struggling wife, who was clinging to his back. Luckily for Smith, the irate husband was no crack shot and the bullets went wide. But Heffridge had another far more potent weapon at his disposal.

'I'll pay a hundred-dollar reward to the man who brings that skunk down.'

The mayor's offer galvanized other bystanders into action. Two or three of the more daring, or maybe drunken, jaspers stepped out into the street ready to claim the reward. Jess Beaman would have loved nothing better than to just stand there howling with laughter at his partner's comic-book antics. But he quickly realized that his intervention was urgently required.

Drawing his own gun, Beaman fired a couple of shots at the feet of those contenders hoping for an easy bonus.

'Better pull back, gents,' he ordered in a calm yet determined drawl, 'if'n you want to meet the next dawn.'

The warning had the desired effect. Two other members of the gang had emerged from the saloon, adding their grim presence to that of the stalwart Beaman. This enabled their panic-stricken leader to mount his horse, which was conveniently placed opposite the door. A couple of shots from an Army Remington quickly removed the fuming mayor from view.

'OK, let's ride, boys,' Beaman hollered, leaping on to his own mount. 'The boss has shot our bolt for keeps in this town.'

A few muted guffaws were instantly silenced as Smith glared around. Forced to ride the full length of the street with his dirty-pink long johns on display was a humiliation that would take a coon's age to live down.

That had been three years before.

But Beaman's associate had not learned from the chastening experience. Other close calls had occurred, although none as mortifying as that in Cimarron.

And here he was, yet again trying his luck. Although

this time, he thankfully appeared to have met his match. As far as Jess Beaman was concerned, women and business were a fatal mix. The two were best kept well apart.

Just then a call from up top announced that they were pulling into Sedona.

TWO

. . . TO SEDONA

The small settlement was little more than an amalgamation of log cabins built around a square for protection against attacks by Indians. White Mountain Apaches were known to frequent the area, led by their much-feared chief, Geronimo.

Unlike the more peaceful Hopi tribe to the north, the Apaches lived up to the meaning of their name, which was 'enemy'. The hostiles resented their tribal lands being invaded by the white-eyes and sought any excuse for exercising that antipathy.

That was one more good reason for the current Overland stage journey having a military escort.

The main block of the trading post was occupied by Axel Roman and his Pima Indian wife, who ran the relay station for the Butterfield Stagecoach Company. A blacksmith's shop, saddlery and, unusually for such a remote enclave, a barber's shop occupied two other sides of the square. Completing the defensive enclave was a large barn and corral where relief horses were kept.

The windows on the outside of the main building had heavy shutters complete with firing holes. This encompassing wooden shield formed a most effective bulwark against any marauding insurgents. So far the few attacks launched against the trading post had been effectively repulsed with no loss of life. The arrival of the unscheduled coach had come as a surprise to the proprietor of the trading post.

'We weren't expecting any fresh arrivals for another two days,' he announced to the driver whilst casting a wary eye at the army patrol. 'Is there something I should know about, Bull?'

The driver went on to explain about the valuable cargo on board.

'In that case, I better get it stashed away in the company safe,' asserted the relay station manager. 'You can't be too careful where gold bullion is concerned.' Assisted by Bull Ferris, he carried the heavy strongbox inside the main building and secured it inside a large iron safe.

The deer carcase was taken away by Roman's wife for preparation using a Pima recipe. Sitting down to the evening meal with their hosts, the tasty venison steaks went down a treat amongst the troopers. There was enough for the passengers as well. And with fresh oranges and cream for dessert, it was indeed a far more appetizing repast than that normally offered to the Overland passengers.

However, John Smith was still intent on ingratiating himself with the delectable Miss Calendar. Beaman sighed. The guy just didn't give up. It was fortunate that Smith was good at managing their business interests or his associate would have quit long before. Nevertheless, Smith's partiality in Beaman's eyes was a weakness they could well do without.

Smith rose from his seat and wandered over to the table that the prospective schoolma'am was sharing with their hosts. Removing his hat, he bowed with a flourish. 'Would you care to join my partner and me for a nightcap, Miss Calendar?' he asked, pasting a lurid smile on to his oily visage. 'I have a bottle of finest French wine that I know ladies of refinement are known to favour.'

The unctuous smile emerged more as a lusty ogle which set Lucy Calendar's teeth on edge. In her most charming voice, she gracefully declined his offer. Without waiting to observe her unwelcome suitor's reaction to the snub, she turned back to continue her conversation with Roman and his wife.

Red-faced, Smith was left inwardly seething as he returned to his own table. His associate could barely contain his amusement.

'That jumped-up bitch is gonna regret knocking me back,' Smith snarled, jabbing his fork into a piece of meat. But for the moment there was nothing he could do about it. They retired earlier than usual as Lieutenant Saunders wanted a dawn start.

Everybody was up at first light the next morning. The troopers were already mounted, awaiting the arrival of their replacements who were coming overland direct from Fort Apache. It was not until the sun had risen over the serrated rim of the Mazatal Mountains that a cloud of dust from the south heralded their appearance.

The starchy officer was less than pleased at having been held up for two hours longer than expected. 'You're late,' he brusquely accused his opposite number, using an arrogant tone to impress his own men. 'And where is Lieutenant Chadwick? I was told he was assigned to take over from me.'

The other officer returned the snappy salute.

'A bunch of renegade bucks have broken out of the San Carlos Reservation and are causing trouble. He's been sent to deal with them,' came the equally forthright reply. 'I'm Lieutenant Squires, his replacement. Me and my men were the only ones available to provide this escort. We only came back off patrol last night. That's why we are late reaching this godforsaken place.'

Saunders responded with a surly grunt. 'Well, it's your responsibility from here to Casa Grande.' He gave the other officer a suspicious look.

Long hair poking beneath his hat was unbecoming to a cavalry officer. And the guy's uniform was slovenly and did not even fit him properly. Saunders shrugged off the unsettling impression about the man. Perhaps being a front-line base, Fort Apache was less exacting when it came to such details. He promised himself to make enquires about this Lieutenant Squires when he returned to Flagstaff.

And with that thought in mind, he swung his mount round and led his own men back in the direction from which they had come the previous day.

'Now we have sorted that out, jump aboard, folks,' urged Bull Ferris. 'There is a heap of miles need burning to reach Casa Grande on time.'

Curly Dick was the only passenger to leave the coach at Sedona. He was heading into the hills to do some lone prospecting.

A cheery wave to the relay station manager, a crack of his trusty bullwhip, and the stagecoach lurched into motion. The six horses snorted and heaved, driven on by the lethal brown serpent that never once touched their straining haunches. Bull Ferris was a past master when it came to getting the most out of his team.

Hollering like a fairground barker, the driver soon had them galloping in unison. The steady rhythm of pounding hoofs provided a comforting sound to the passengers.

For the first half-hour after they left Sedona behind, Smith chatted away as if nothing untoward had occurred to put a damper on his relationship with the other passengers. General talk ensued, concerning all manner of subjects.

Favoured topics were the weather and teaching methods currently employed in the classroom. That was for Miss Calendar's benefit. Gandy tried raising the issue of rising liquor prices but was ignored. Even the latest clothing fashions, advertised in society journals and currently finding their way into the frontier towns, were discussed.

The easy-going chatter lulled the girl into a false sense of bonhomie. The bone drummer consoled himself by falling asleep. The effects of too much French wine the night before helped in that respect.

Then, out of the blue, everything suddenly changed.

It began with Jess Beaman leaning out the window and signalling to one of the accompanying troopers. The man acknowledged the gesture with a curt nod and spurred ahead. Moments later a gruff shout could be heard from outside.

'Haul up those reins, driver,' came the taut demand. 'This is a stick-up.'

The snappy stipulation was accompanied by two pistol shots. The passengers heard a croak of pain followed moments later by a dull thud as a body hit the ground. It was Raccoon Adler who had made the mistake of resisting the challenge.

Another shot followed seconds later.

Miss Calendar leaned out of the window. What she perceived brought a fearful scream to her lips. The guard was lying on the ground next to the mountain man. Blood poured from the fatal wounds. Three-Fingered Jimmy Dean had made his final run for the Butterfield Stagecoach Company.

The next razor-edged order was aimed at Bull Ferris. 'You can go join your buddy and the other fool, driver. Or co-operate and throw down that strongbox.'

Ferris certainly was no weak-willed mincer. His leathery features tightened with anger. But he realized that any resistance on his part would be suicidal. Bull was not ready to strum a harp with the angels yet awhile.

And he had every intention of drawing his pension at the end of the year when he retired.

The girl drew back inside the coach, appealing to Smith and his associate for help. That was when she received a second shock. Coming face to face with two drawn revolvers drained the colour from her cheeks. Evil grins split both the faces of the two men sitting opposite. It was Beaman who enlightened the stunned female.

'Meet Dutch Henry Vandyke, lady,' he declared, pointing to his partner. 'And we're here to rob the stage of its valuable cargo.'

The girl's upper lip trembled as she tried to make sense of the dire situation that had suddenly invaded her gentle world. 'B-but the s-soldiers,' she stammered. 'They are meant to prevent this from happening.'

'And they would have too,' replied the thoroughly animated gang leader, 'if'n my boys hadn't changed places with them.'

At that moment, the officer known as Lieutenant Squires rode up to the coach and peered in through the window. He removed his hat. Lank dark hair cascaded around his shoulders as he bowed to the lone female occupant of the coach.

Dutch turned to address the newcomer. 'Everything go according to plan, Lieutenant?' He smirked for the girl's benefit. 'The lady here reckons you and the boys should be guarding the gold bullion not stealing it.'

Trigger Wixx threw back his head and roared with laughter. 'It sure did, boss. Your plan worked like a dream. And she's right about us guarding the gold.

Don't you fret, lady, we'll keep our eyes on it . . . until it's exchanged for greenbacks.'

THREE

BLUECOAT BLUES

While Dutch Henry and Beaman were keeping an eye on things as stagecoach passengers, the other five members of the Vandyke gang had picked up the trail of the relieving escort. Once it had left Fort Apache, the patrol took the route through the Mazatal Mountains following the left bank of Tonto Creek.

It was a little-used trail but would cut two days off the longer way north through Salt River Canyon. The gang rode parallel to the patrol, keeping a weather eye on them from high up on the Sierra Ancha ridge.

When shadows began to lengthen, heralding the approach of dusk, Trigger Wixx called a halt for them to make camp for the night. It was he who had been put in charge of the operation. And Dutch Henry's orders had been unequivocal.

'I don't care how you do it,' he had iterated. 'Just make darned sure that none of them blue-bellies escape to raise the alarm.'

Dismounting, the gang studied the army camp from their elevated position on the lofty ridge. Any attempt to get down there and attack the patrol would surely make enough noise to alert the Devil himself. This was an operation for guile and cunning.

And Wixx had the very man for the job.

Sharp features and a long wispy moustache gave Foggy Duke the distinct resemblance to a desert rat. Wixx smiled at the wizened features. But he acknowledged that Duke was the ideal man for this assignment. He had been a Shadow during the War, one of those will o' the wisps who could sneak into a camp, despatch an opponent and disappear like a ghost. He was also an expert with a knife.

Calling the outlaw over, he explained what had to be done.

'Take one other man with you,' Wixx concluded. 'The rest of us will keep watch from up here. If'n it proves too much of a problem, don't take any risks. Get back. Then we'll figure out some other way to get rid of them.'

But Duke was confident of being able to handle the task. He chose a hefty dude to accompany him. On first impressions, Buckey Sontag appeared to be an ungainly, lumbering oaf who would create more of racket than a Thanksgiving hoo-ha. But Duke knew that his buddy was reliable, a good man to have on your side.

Not only that, he was lethal when it came to unarmed combat. Sontag had learned the martial skills from

Chinese coolies while working with the Union Pacific railroad construction gangs.

He was a silent killing machine.

The mismatched pair looked like a variety show double act. But appearances can be deceptive. Wixx was confident that the two old buddies would carry out their task with military efficiency.

Unaware of the humour they had aroused in their associates, the pair of man hunters set off on their mission. They dropped down into the serried ranks of ponderosa pine. Eager eyes followed their progress until the dense tree cover swallowed them up.

The soldiers had made camp on a flat terrace beside the creek. Their fire provided a beacon towards which the hunters were able to home in. A guard had been established on the edge of the campsite near where the horses were picketed. The other troopers were gathered around the fire.

It took a good half-hour to pick a safe passage down the steep flanks of the valley. Stony and loose underfoot amidst the ranks of conifer growth, this was not a trip that could have been safely accomplished in a hurry, nor on horseback. On reaching the floor of the valley, the pair crept silently towards where the first guard had taken up his position.

Having been in the army during the war, Duke was fully cognizant of army procedures. He knew that the watch operated on a four-hour cycle. The first stand was at eight in the evening. That was too early for the outlaws. They needed the troopers to settle down for the night before attacking.

But Duke was wary of going up against five hardened troopers so he decided to take them out one at a time.

As the midnight hour drew near, he signalled to his buddy that the moment had arrived to make their lethal play. The first task was to remove the sentry.

They had agreed on the plan of action while maintaining their vigil. The wait had presented no difficulties for the deadly duo. Each was well versed in the art of patience when stalking their prey. During the war, Duke had often been called upon to keep watch for long periods, sometimes days at a time. He was able to shut his mind down whilst still remaining alert.

Leaving Sontag, he circled around behind where the horses were picketed. Once in position, he deliberately made them snicker. This alerted the sentry, who had been leaning against a tree smoking a cigarette. Instantly alert, the guy stubbed out the butt and moved across to see what had bothered the mounts. With his attention fully occupied at the front, Sontag then crept up behind him.

He was surprisingly nimble on his feet for such a big man. That was another reason Foggy Duke had selected him. Making nary a sound, the big man encircled the sentry's neck with a thick, sinewy arm. It quickly tightened, cutting off any cry of alarm. The man's eyes bulged. His rifle fell to the ground. A swift jerk to the left resulted in a crisp snap and the guard slumped down, his neck broken.

It was a clean kill and brought a twisted grimace to the killer's rough features.

'I couldn't have done that better myself,' whispered

an impressed Foggy Duke as he rejoined his sidekick. 'Now all we have to do is wait for his replacement to turn up. Reckon we should pull the same stunt again?' The army veteran looked to his buddy for agreement.

Sontag gave a curt nod. Being almost twice the size of the rat-faced Duke, Sontag easily manhandled the heavyweight corpse of the dead trooper into the cover of the trees. They did not have long to wait for the other man to arrive.

The yawning trooper made no effort to conceal his approach. After all, why should he? There was no reason to suppose any danger threatened. The Apache didn't engage in night travelling. And who else would be lurking in this remote wilderness at midnight?

Private Eli Patch scratched himself and stretched his stiff limbs. A peevish grumble issued from his throat. He had been awakened from a deep sleep by that durned greenhorn officer.

Patch had been dreaming about the fun he was going to have with that latest addition to Molly Mitchell's Hen House. Fort Apache tolerated the den of ill-repute as it kept the troopers happy. A doctor regularly inspected the soiled doves to ensure they were free from unwholesome diseases likely to contaminate the soldiers.

Patch stumbled into the clearing. He rubbed his eyes, trying to pierce the stygian gloom. The sentry he was replacing was nowhere to be seen.

'You taking a leak, Jaybird?' he called out. A muted response came from over by the horses. Patch sniggered. 'Fasten up, then, and I'll take over.' He walked across to check on the picket line.

As previously, Buckey Sontag emerged from behind a tree and cat-footed up behind the oblivious bluecoat. But this time his heavy boot stepped on a dry twig. The sharp crack delivered a warning to Private Patch that all was not as it should be. He swung round on his heel. On seeing the burly thug sneaking up behind him, he reacted with the precision drilled into every trooper by their training sergeant. The Springfield rifle came up ready to deliver its lethal charge.

Sontag was taken by surprise. His reactions were stilted. For a brief moment the two antagonists stared at one another. Patch's mouth opened to yell out a warning to his sleeping companions. All seemed lost for Buckey Sontag and the plan of eliminating the army patrol.

It was Foggy Duke who saved the day.

Stepping into the open from behind the picket line, he launched a Bowie knife with a fluid, over-handed sweep. It was a pure reflex action. The deadly blade winged across the intervening stretch. Traces of moonlight glinted off the polished steel as it buried its razored point into the back of Private Eli Patch.

The soldier threw up his hands and slumped to the ground.

Sontag breathed a heavy sigh of relief. His heart was pumping like a Comanche war drum. That had been a close call and no mistake.

'Where in thunder did you learn a trick like that?' he croaked out in awed respect for the little man's skilled manoeuvre.

'A necessary piece of cunning when you run with Bloody Bill Anderson,' he replied shortly. Everybody knew about the ruthless exploits of the notorious Confederate guerrilla fighter and his band of cut-throats. Foggy Duke had been his chief sniper when it came to infiltrating enemy lines. 'Now shift that corpse into the undergrowth to join his buddy. There are still three more to be dealt with. And we have to make sure their uniforms are not messed up.'

A new respect for the little man showed in the burly outlaw's demeanour as Sontag hefted the body into cover. The two outlaws discarded the Springfields in favour of their own much more lethal Winchester repeaters.

Quietly they moved through the tree cover like a couple of wraiths. Duke signalled a halt at the edge of the clearing where the troopers had made camp.

One of them was on his feet. His high-crowned army Stetson indicated that he was the officer in charge. It was his duty to ensure that each change of the guard was carried out to the letter of army regulations. And this being his first assignment, Lieutenant Alfred Chadwick was making sure that no corners were cut.

When the trooper known as Jaybird did not return to camp, Chadwick started to get worried. He paced about the camp, hands grasped behind his back as he peered into the dense night enclosing the camp. But any attempt to pierce the shroud of blackness proved to be ineffectual.

He frowned. Something wasn't right.

Were these men playing tricks – trying to make him

look foolish being a new replacement? Well, he was having none of that. If'n they were up to no good, he would personally flay their miserable hides with a bull-whip.

But somehow, he didn't reckon that this bunch of dimwits would have the nerve to bait an officer, even a greenhorn fresh out of the military academy. Then another thought burst in on his cogitations.

Perhaps there was a rampant grizzly out there.

'On your feet, men!' he rapped out to the two recumbent bodies beside the fire. The sleepy forms struggled out of their blankets and staggered to their feet. 'Does either of you know why Jaybird has not returned from his turn at sentry duty on the picket line?'

The wavering demand was uttered in a deliberately firm crackle to hide the officer's nervousness. The sinister hooting of an owl did nothing to stiffen his resolve.

The two remaining men looked at each other. Bafflement registered on their obtuse faces. Shoulders lifted in listless shrugs. Chadwick scowled in frustration. What should he do? The three of them just stood there beside the fire, their gun belts forgotten and lying on the ground.

The young officer was given no opportunity to tackle his first problem.

All of a sudden, gunfire erupted from the edge of the clearing.

Silhouetted against the flickering light cast by the camp fire, the three soldiers made perfect targets. They didn't stand a chance. The pair of bushwhackers unleashed a rapid-fire salvo of hot lead from which no mortal could have escaped. Orange tongues of flame ripped apart the tranquil serenity of the Tonto Basin.

The victims of the killing spree twitched and danced in the grim halo of orange light. They presented a tableau of demented fiends acting out a diabolic show from Hell. Fountains of red spewed from numerous fatal wounds.

As quickly as it had started, the gruesome execution was cut short. A macabre silence ensued. Duke was the first to emerge from the dark fringes of the encircling gloom. Gun pointing at the fallen bodies, he approached them with an innate caution born of experience.

The two men toed the still forms. There was no response. They had done their work with consummate aplomb. The rattish outlaw's wizened face split in a mirthless smile of satisfaction. Without further ado, he snatched a blazing log from the fire and waved it over his head. It was a signal to those waiting on the ridge that the job had been successfully accomplished.

Buckey Sontag poured himself a cup of coffee from the large pot that had been left for the sentries returning from duty. He also helped himself to a warming corndog.

'Let's make ourselves comfortable,' he suggested to his partner. 'We can't move out until morning. And these guys won't be needing any more of these vittles.'

Duke wandered across to join him. He threw the branch back on to the fire.

'While we're here,' he suggested, 'we might as well

34

see what dough they're carrying. The boss won't begrudge us a little bonus for all our trouble.'

Sontag nodded his agreement to the proposal. Both men were indifferent to the deadly display they had so recently delivered. 'I'll go check those two dudes on the picket line,' he said, tossing the dregs of his cup on to the fire. 'OK if'n we split the take fifty-fifty?'

'Suits me,' agreed Duke.

Following a lucrative search of all the saddle-packs and bodies, the cool pair of killers pocketed their loot. They then sat down to enjoy the meal left by the recent occupants of the camp.

The bloody corpses bothered them not a jot. It was a job well done.

Following a hearty supper, the two men built up the fire against any wandering predators that might be in the vicinity. A couple of high-class cigars from the officer's knapsack with a nip of Scotch whiskey from his hip flask and they were ready for settling down. Their consciences immune from any feeling of remorse for the heinous crime, sleep came easy.

As the false dawn lightened the eastern sky with its orange glow, Foggy Duke stretched the stiffness from his limbs. Shrugging off his blanket, he stoked up the dying embers of the fire to reheat the coffee pot. There was nothing better than a cup of hot strong Arbuckles to set a man up for the day.

The first job for the two men was to strip the uniforms off the corpses. Any bloodstains were washed out of the material. The bullet holes would have to be sewn up once they reached the gang's hideout in the Santa

Catalina mountains.

Wandering wolf packs and other wild creatures would soon dispose of the dead bodies. Any other equipment was scattered amongst the rocks adjoining Tonto Creek. Nobody was likely to come this way for some time, even when the disappearance of the patrol was investigated.

The final task was to release the horses into the wild. Freed from their human encumbrances, they galloped off along the creek.

'These nags will sniff out one of the wild herds that roam these mountains,' Duke informed his partner.

'Guess we're doing them a favour, then,' added the heavyweight Sontag.

'Ain't we the thoughtful types?' his little buddy smirked.

The outlaws took a final look around the camp site before tramping back up the side of the valley to rejoin Trigger Wixx and the rest of the gang.

FOUR

CASA GRANDE

The sheriff of Casa Grande plumped himself down in his favourite chair and picked up a pile of freshly delivered Wanted posters. The face of Dutch Henry Vandyke stared back at him.

A serious frown crossed the lawman's rugged features. It was a pen-portrait of the notorious outlaw whose bounty had gone up yet again. Chad Gleeson rolled a cigarette. Scratching a vesta on the scarred desk top, he lit up and drew hard on the white tube. Tendrils of smoke dribbled from between pursed lips.

This was the third time in as many months that a dodger for the infamous owl hoot had landed on his desk. Vandyke and his gang were causing mayhem throughout the territory. And thus far, nobody had gotten close to halting their depredations.

Few people had ever seen the Dutchman's face. Gleeson's concentrated gaze tried unsuccessfully to

37

penetrate the artistic depiction. The drawing could have applied to anybody. But the list of his crimes outlined beneath the sketch was certainly no fictitious account. Robbery with violence, murder, kidnapping and rustling had made the Vandyke gang the most feared in the south west.

His faced hardened, the full mouth tightening to a thin line of gritty determination. Chad Gleeson's mission to capture the outlaw was personal.

The lawman's attention was distracted by high-spirited yelling outside in the street. He looked up in time to see a pair of riders galloping past his office. Blazing sixguns were accompanied by raucous shouts of glee.

An audible sigh of frustration rumbled in his throat. He knew exactly who was responsible. It had to be those dumbbells, Jones and Prieta. The two cowpokes had been warned the previous week about racing their horses in town.

Chad Gleeson, better known as Seven-Up because of his penchant for the popular card game, always believed that every miscreant should be given a second chance. These critters had ignored the warning and would pay the price for their foolhardiness. He lurched to his feet and grabbed a shotgun from the rack. Slamming his battered plainsman atop the thatch of sandy hair, he stamped out of the office.

Pedestrians had been forced to fling themselves out of the way of the hurtling competitors. Gleeson gritted his teeth. Serious injuries could result from such reckless behaviour.

Quickly stepping down on to the rutted thoroughfare,

he took up a position in the middle of the street. The lethal twelve-gauge Greener was in full view. At the end of Main, the two contenders swung around eager for the final leg of their race. The winner had to pay for the services of Sarah May, the most delectable of Madame Syn's calico queens.

Urging their mounts to a frenetic gallop, the racers jockeyed for position, each bent low and hugging their horses' necks.

'Best be careful you don't bite that poor gal with those fangs of your'n,' Prieta joshed his buddy. 'Madam Syn might charge you extra.'

'It's gonna be you that pays up,' countered Squirrel-Tooth Jones with a scoff while urging his mount ahead.

The jovial banter had distracted the racers. Neither saw the lone figure standing in the street.

His gambler's face set in a rigid grimace, Seven-Up waited until they were fifty yards away. Then he let fly with both barrels into the air. The ear-shattering blast brought the careering racers to an ungainly halt. Their mounts reared up on hind legs. The sudden upset to their irresponsible contest found the pair unceremoniously tipped off'n their saddles into the dust.

Gleeson casually strolled up to them.

'On your feet, boys!' he rapped out. 'There's a nice uncomfortable lodging in the jailhouse for you pair of jugheads.' The two youngsters scrambled to their feet rubbing sore heads. 'Now shift your asses!'

The humiliated cowpokes hobbled across the street encouraged by the sheriff's jabbing gun. Numerous bystanders muttered to one another. Some hurled brazen suggestions of what punishment should be administered to such reckless louts.

'Tie 'em to a wagon wheel and give the fools a taste of the lash,' shouted one irate citizen.

'They should be ashamed of themselves,' chirped a waspish harridan, setting her hat straight. 'What would their mothers think of such outrageous behaviour?'

Gleeson ignored the spirited comments.

Once inside the office, he wasted no time in prodding the two rannies through into the cell block at the rear.

'You clowns ought to know better than racing broncs along Main Street,' he rasped, ushering the two men into the first cell. Slamming the iron door closed, he twisted the key. It grated harshly in the rusty old lock.

It was round-up time for the ranches surrounding the southern Arizona town – a busy period when all hands were fully occupied. The two cowboys hung their heads. Their miserable expressions were partly on account of thick heads due to an overindulgence of hard liquor that had prompted the rash bet – but more because their pay would be docked.

Racing cayuses within the town limits was against the law and punishable by two weeks in the slammer.

'Your boss ain't gonna be too pleased about having a couple of his boys stuck in the pokey at this time of year.' The woebegone prisoners merely groaned as the sheriff wandered back into the main office.

His remark was a dry-witted understatement. Ranch owner Harvey Proctor who operated an outfit called the Rising Sun would be positively fuming when he learned of the misdemeanour. If'n he wanted the two men released, it would cost him twenty bucks apiece.

Frank Jones and his buddy Chickweed Prieta knew that the fines would come out of their wages. That is if'n the boss didn't fire them. Plenty of drifters passed through Pima County looking for work at round-up time.

They slumped down on to the grubby bunks. Any regrets they felt for their rash indiscretion had come too late.

Satisfied with the action taken, Seven-Up hustled outside to catch up with one of the other Rising Sun hands. Cabrio Vamori, Proctor's Mexican ramrod, had also witnessed the fracas and was stumping down the boardwalk. A grim cast on the swarthy round face hinted at his evident exasperation with the two hands.

'Tell your boss that Jones and Prieta will be my guests for the next two weeks unless he forks out their fine.'

Vamori shook his head. 'In saloon I tell those *idiotos* to be careful,' mumbled the ramrod. 'But they are hot-heads. Boss will be chewing leather when he finds out.'

Gleeson shrugged. It was not his call, although he didn't envy the Mexican cowboy's task of passing on the unwelcome tidings. He wandered back to the office and sank into a chair outside. Rolling another stogie, he lit up and gratefully inhaled the smoke. It tasted good.

Resting his boots on the boardwalk rail, he watched the town settle down, hopefully for a period of calm.

'Morning, sheriff.'

The perky greeting came from a fussy little woman of

41

middle age. A neat feathered hat was perched atop a bun of thick grey hair. Steel-rimmed spectacles gave her the appearance of a wise owl. Not a bad description of Hettie Pierce, Gleeson surmised.

The spinster ran a small emporium called Rainbow World. It was the most popular establishment with all the kids in town. That was because Hettie sold all manner of candy bars and sweet confectionery. Her shopfront was painted in a variety of colours to match the products within.

Seven-Up tipped his hat.

'That was very brave of you to confront those two drunken cowboys.' A hint of esteem was conveyed in the shopkeeper's approbation. 'You could easily have been run down by those roughnecks.'

'The law has to be upheld, Miss Pierce,' he replied with nonchalant composure.

Hettie coughed, giving herself chance to voice the notion that was uppermost in her mind. And not only hers. All the members of the Casa Grande Ladies Temperance League were on tenterhooks regarding the intentions of the alluring lawman.

'When is a handsome young man like yourself going to get hitched?' she asked.

This was a question the League had discussed at length since the tall Texan was appointed to the job of sheriff six months before. Hettie was the first to express it aloud. Being a maiden lady of advancing years, it had been suggested that such a query coming from her would not be misconstrued.

Thus far Seven-Up Chad Gleeson had shown more

inclination to dally in the saloon at the green baize tables than with members of the opposite sex.

'All in good time, Hettie,' he answered, concealing a wry smirk. 'All in good time.'

It was a neutral response that gave nothing away. The sheriff had enjoyed numerous affiliations during his thirty-two years. But the right lady had yet to come along with whom he felt able to settle down in domestic harmony. Being a lawman on the western frontier did not sit well with family life.

Miss Pierce was persistent in her endeavour to probe beneath the taciturn exterior. 'Did you know that we are getting a new schoolteacher?' she said.

Gleeson remained tight-lipped. His eyebrows lifted. He assumed the new arrival would be female. Probably one of those straight-laced starchy types with her beaky snout stuck in the clouds when not in a dusty book.

Much to the sheriff's relief, the Overland stage rumbled into view at the end of the street. It was that special he had heard about. This was a good opportunity to stymie any further inquest into his matrimonial plans. He stood up.

'Time I met the stage, Miss Pierce,' he said, moving briskly away.

The bustling proprietor of Rainbow World was left open-mouthed and with nothing to impart to her friends. It was most unsatisfactory. With a shake of the head, she scurried off to reopen her store.

Straight away, Gleeson sensed that things were not right.

Where was the guard he would have expected to be

riding shotgun? And there was no military escort. Increasing his pace, the sheriff crossed the street as the rattling vehicle shuddered to an undignified halt.

Dust rose in an angry cloud surrounding the driver, who leapt off the bench and hurried into the Butterfield depot.

A solitary passenger was left to emerge unaided.

'What happened, Mr?' enquired the sheriff, helping the flustered man retrieve his battered luggage from the overhead rack.

'The stage was robbed,' spluttered the distraught man. 'It was Dutch Henry and his gang. They must have murdered the real escort of troopers and taken their place. The skunks were after the gold bullion. But worst of all—' The little man paused, swallowing nervously as the gruesome experience was replayed in his distraught mind. Then he slung a thumb back to the coach. '— they killed the guard and the roof passenger. They're both inside. The stench in there is some'n awful.'

He leaned over the hitching rail and puked his guts into the street. Gleeson ignored the poor man's distress.

'What happened to the new schoolma'am?' he exclaimed.

Hyram Gandy took some moment to recover his composure. Then he shook his head. 'They abducted Miss Calendar.' A nervous guffaw rumbled in his throat. 'That gal sure weren't no dowdy spinster, sheriff. A better looking gal I've yet to set eyes on. That's why Dutch Henry took her.'

The sheriff gave the drummer a quizzical frown.

'He'd been giving her the glad eye ever since we left Flagstaff. The rat told us that his name was Smith.' Gandy shrugged. 'Nobody has reckoned to have ever seen his face so we fell in with the charade. He won't be able to pull that stunt anymore now. I could describe every line and crease on that skunk's kisser.' He finished with a sarcastic grunt. 'Even down to the pomade he wears.'

'You'll need to come across to the office after you're settled in at the hotel, Mr Gandy,' the sheriff informed the drummer. 'The Crystal Ball puts clean sheets on the beds. I'll be needing a full statement of what happened.'

'Be glad to, sheriff,' snarled Gandy. 'Those critters scattered all my samples to the four winds. I'm gonna have to wire head office in Denver for some replacements. They could take a month to arrive. And during that time I'm stuck here forced to live off what little savings I have.'

The somewhat unkempt salesman was none too pleased. He extracted a hip flask from his back pocket and put it to his lips. It was empty.

'But first I need another drink.'

The drummer lurched off up the street in the direction of the Tomahawk Saloon. A lurid notice had caught his attention. It read: *Half-Price Drinks For One Day Only!*

Gleeson watched the inebriated drummer weave a tortuous course along the boardwalk. After assimilating the full details of the raid from Bull Ferris, he wandered back to his office. It was late in the day. So there was no chance of organizing a posse to pursue the robbers until the next morning.

It would give him chance to read that Wanted poster and learn more about Dutch Henry and the Vandyke Gang.

FIVE

NO LUCK FOR
SEVEN-UP

Deep within the Catalina mountains, the Vandyke Gang
were resting up. Dutch Henry had taken over an abandoned miner's cabin located beside Horseshoe Springs.
It was one of many such ravines rippling through the
craggy enclave known as Laughing Buzzard Canyon.
And to this unknown alien landscape he always
returned following each of the gang's numerous forays.

Remote from the outside world, it enabled the gang
to relax without having the law breathing down their
necks. It also enabled their leader to split the loot and
plan their next job. He had hinted that once they
cashed in the gold bullion for US dollars, a vacation was
due to them all.

The idea suggested was that they split up and head
their separate ways, meeting up at some future date to

resume their lawless activities.

On this occasion, however, the situation was different.

Dutch now had a girl in tow. She was still giving him the cold shoulder. But the gang boss was not giving up. The more she spurned his rather inept advances, the greater became the outlaw leader's determination to break down her obdurate willpower. Dutch was convinced that his innate charm and good looks would eventually reap rich rewards. Then she would be eating out of his hand.

Until then, he would bide his time.

The rest of the gang were none too impressed. The girl was holding them back. Her presence had dimmed their natural exuberance regarding the forthcoming vacation. By this time they should have been well on their way to the Mexican border to get rid of their latest haul.

Revolutionaries who were eager to overthrow the existing government had agreed to pay good money for the gold bullion. It was worth far more to them than the Mexican paper currency then in circulation.

Mutterings of discontent had been voiced. The gang knew that the army would be after them this time on account of the ruthless slaying of the patrol. They were eager to head south for the border, and safety. But any murmurings of dissatisfaction concerning the girl's presence were only disseminated amongst themselves.

The Dutchman had a notoriously violent temper when riled.

The fate of Latigo Chavez was still fresh in their

minds. Only the previous month, the Mexican gun-slinger had questioned Vandyke's choice of silk vest, claiming it was too gaudy and made his eyes sore. The gang had been drinking in a saloon in the lawless pan-handle town of Hooker. Chavez had arrived late. His remark had only been meant as a joke.

Dutch had not said a word, just looked at him stony-faced while gently rubbing the scar on his face. Then he had casually drawn his revolver and emptied the whole cylinder. When the smoke dispersed, the bandit was lying dead on the saloon floor in a spreading pool of his own blood.

Lawless anarchy was rife in the narrow strip of ungoverned territory. But Dutch Henry's brutally feral reaction would be talked about for years to come.

Only Jess Beaman had the authority to voice any dissent at bringing the girl along. His carefully phrased reservations had met with a brick wall. Vandyke was adamant that the girl went with them to Mexico.

So that was that. No more discussion on the issue.

Two of the men expressed a desire to visit the nearest town of Jacaranda. Their suggestion to stock up on some more liquor and other desirables that the gang needed while stuck in the hideout received general approval. They all looked to Vandyke for his agree-ment.

The arrogant gang boss sucked on a cigar, a thought-ful expression tugged at the itchy scar running down the left side of his face. To some men the pale blemish would have been a hindrance to their success with the dames. Where Dutch Henry was concerned, they loved him all the more for the knife wound.

A much elaborated tale of how he was ambushed by a skulking roughneck in Denver always elicited their sympathy. The subsequent besting of the treacherous skunk likewise received hearty approval, accompanied by more physical rewards.

Following the tense period of deliberation, a nod of approval found his men relaxing.

'And while you boys are there,' he said, handing over a wad of banknotes, 'get me some fancy bauble for the lady.'

'What sort do you want, boss?' enquired a stocky jasper named Slim Jim Bonita.

'Use your imagination,' huffed Dutch with a sour grimace. He threw his arms wide in frustration. His patience with the snooty schoolteacher was beginning to wear thin. 'A necklace, bangle, whatever will make that stuffy dame crack a smile for once.'

Bonita suppressed a grin of his own. He nodded, accepting the dough, then gestured to his partner that he was ready to leave.

Next morning, Chad Gleeson began circulating around Casa Grande asking for volunteers to make up a posse. But as soon as the name of Dutch Henry Vandyke was mentioned, the shutters went down. The wholesale killing of the army patrol had unnerved the whole town. These were varmints who would have no hesitation in gunning down anybody who tried to arrest them.

All manner of excuses were put forward to save face.

Once the word had gone round that the sheriff was looking for men to join a posse, people suddenly crossed the street to avoid any confrontation. He finally managed to gain a captive audience by entering the Good Will Chophouse.

On seeing the lawman standing inside the door, the scrape of crockery on plates and the hum of conversation faded to a tense silence. Gleeson noticed that two of them were members of the council. A probing eye fastened on to the two diners. But they looked away, anxious not to meet his probing gaze.

'You all know why I'm here,' he announced firmly.

The silence was heavier than a Brahman bull. Only the house cat could be heard mewing under a table.

'This dude has a hefty price on his head,' the sheriff went on further stressing, 'and his men will also be worth more than you guys earn in a month of Sundays. Ain't that worth a few days on the trail?'

'What darned use is it being the richest corpse in the graveyard?' iterated Bernie Stoker, who was the Mayor of Casa Grande as he forked a lump of bacon into his mouth. 'We are just simple folks trying to make a living, not cold-blood gunslingers.'

There was a general murmur of agreement amongst the others.

'If'n it had been the town's money that had been stolen,' interposed the other councillor. Jacob Randle was a butcher and had taken courage from his associate to voice his own fears. 'You might have more luck. But this ain't our affair, sheriff.'

'What about the woman who was kidnapped?'

51

snapped Gleeson angrily. 'She was going to teach your kids.'

There was no answer to that. The timid diners turned away to hide their red faces. Their minds were made up and no amount of threats or cajoling was going to shift them. The sheriff threw them a look of scornful disdain and stamped out.

Maybe he would have better luck in the Tomahawk.

A belt of thunder rumbled across the leaden sky. Terrified by the loud crash, a ragged dog flew across the sheriff's path. Heavy drops of rain began to fall, bouncing on the hard-packed earth of the street. It matched the grim mood of the lawman as he stepped briskly towards the saloon.

Inside the Tomahawk he only found two men ready to accept his proposal. Neither of whom was suitable.

One was Bitterroot Kearney who acted as the saloon swamper. He barely knew one end of his mop from the other, let alone a gun. The second was Hyram Gandy who appeared to have been in the saloon all night judging by his dishevelled appearance and slurred speech. He raised a glass, almost falling off his chair.

Gleeson did not even acknowledge their offers.

The morose lawman drifted back to the jailhouse. What sort of a town was this? Not a single able-bodied man was prepared to help bring these owl hoots to justice. He vented his spleen by spitting into the muddy street. The rain went unheeded.

Stamping into the office, the familiar smell of gun oil and coffee assailed his nostrils. A fastidious lawman, Chad Gleeson always ensured that his armoury was kept in working order. Rifles, shotguns and revolvers were locked away in a rack over on the right wall. He wandered across to the ever-present bubbling coffee pot on the stove.

The need for a solid jolt of strong Arbuckles was denied him when a raucous holler came from the cell block.

'What time do you serve up breakfast in this hotel, sheriff?'

The sardonic retort from Chickweed Prieta received a hearty chortle from his buddy. Frank Jones added his own witty postscript. 'Make mine a double helping of hash browns and have the cook fry the bacon extra crispy.'

If'n they had to spend time in the hoosegow, might as well have some fun at the expense of that killjoy tin star.

Seven-Up snorted. Those two conceited cowpokes had clearly shrugged off their recent embarrassing arrest and were venting their displeasure at being holed up.

'Don't forget, sheriff, we like our coffee nice and strong with plenty of sugar.'

Gleeson's face assumed a purple hue. His blood was up. Not only was the darned town full of lily-livered wet blankets, he now had to listen to the noisy bleating of his prisoners. Well, he was having none of it. He shook the rainwater from his hat, suddenly realizing how wet he was. That only soured his mood even more.

Grabbing up a horsewhip, he cracked it loudly and headed for the cells. A demonic leer twisted the hand-some features into an alien grimace. It was against all the solid lawman's principles to mistreat prisoners. But on this occasion he could be forgiven for exercising some much-needed physical punishment, if only to strike the fear of God into this pair of knuckleheads.

It would certainly make Seven-Up Chad Gleeson feel a sight better.

He was about to open the cellblock door when his guardian angel intervened. What was he doing? The storm of insanity must have clouded his judgement and drowned out the normally tolerant personality. He paused, struggling to shake off the manic feeling. Thankfully the Devil's invitation had been restrained just in time.

Slowly the red mist dissolved, allowing wisdom and good sense to prevail. A light shone out of the darkness of his torment, revealing the answer to his dilemma. The whip was discarded. Now he knew there was another way by which this charade could be turned to his advantage.

In the blink of an eye, Gleeson's face changed from dour depression to grinning enthusiasm. The scheme he had in mind was pure genius.

He went through into the cellblock where the simpering pair of arrogant puppies were all set to continue their harassment. But the smirking face that accosted them brought puzzled looks of dismay to the youthful countenances.

Gleeson crossed his arms, his legs purposefully astride.

'I have a proposition for you boys,' he declared, fixing a gritty peeper on to each of the nonplussed duo.

'What are you offering, sheriff?' enquired an intrigued Chickweed Prieta. 'Some extra helpings of apple pie?'

The sheriff ignored the jibe. His menacing smile sent a tremor of anxiety down the kid's spine. Then he delivered his proposal.

'I need a couple of guys that are handy with their guns and used to hard riding, maybe for days on end,' he said. 'Being Rising Sun hands and well respected by your boss, I am accepting you two as volunteers to help me catch Dutch Henry and his gang. You will receive the usual fee for being a member of the posse.'

'I thought you said this was a proposition?' grumbled a sceptical Frank Jones through his prominent front choppers. 'That sounds like we ain't got much choice.'

'There's always a choice, kid,' smirked Gleeson. 'So what do you say?'

'No way!' protested Squirrel-Tooth. 'We ain't going after that crazy galoot for no pesky few bucks.'

'We'd rather stay here and take our chances,' added Prieta. 'And keep our skins in one piece.'

'That sure is a pity,' chided Gleeson, shaking his head in a mocking reflection. 'About the whole skin, I mean. 'Cos I hear tell that Harvey Proctor is a right tartar when it comes to dealing with hands who stupidly get themselves locked up. The last one found himself tied to a wagon wheel and had his back flayed with a bull whip.'

Prieta gulped. His eyes bulged. It was before his time on the Rising Sun. But he'd heard the story.

Seven-Up knew when he was holding an ace hand.

'And if'n you don't see fit to join up, I'm going to rec-
ommend you stay in jail until the circuit judge arrives.
Now that will be . . .' He tapped his head in thought.
'Yep, I reckon it'll be two months at least. And I'll also
advocate that he fine you each a couple of hundred
bucks.'

The prisoners gulped. Their cocky manner had been
crushed.

The sheriff quickly capitalized on his advantage.
'Times are tough at the moment, boys. And we can only
afford to feed prisoners on the leavings from the diner.
That is if'n there is anything left in the chophouse each
evening. If not,' – he shrugged – 'guess you'll have to
tighten your belts. You fellas are in for a lean spell.'

This time it was Squirrel-Tooth's turn to look ashen-
faced. A film of sweat broke out on the young punk's
forehead.

'On the other hand . . .' Chad was enjoying himself
immensely. He knew that the two were on the verge of
capitulating. Now it was time to play his ace in the hole.
'Come in with me and I'll promise you an even share in
all the reward money. Now that could easily amount to
a few grand, maybe more.'

The two cowpokes looked at one another and
nodded.

'OK, sheriff, it's a deal,' they both said together.

'I thought you might cotton to that notion,' Gleeson
replied, maintaining a straight face. 'And I'll make sure
that your boss knows what a pair of gutsy rannigans he
has on his payroll.'

SIX

JACKED OFF IN JACARANDA

It was an hour later that the unlikely posse set out on their mission from Casa Grande. Numerous eyes watched their progress down the street. Only Hettie Pierce came out to wish them luck.

'I'd join up with you myself if'n I could use a gun, sheriff,' the feisty woman sniffed, aiming an accusatory eye at the sullen-faced onlookers. 'Unlike some I could mention around here.'

Chad acknowledged her good wishes with a smile.

Then, setting his dour face to the front, the lawman looked neither to right nor left as the makeshift posse trotted past the various establishments. His opinion regarding the good citizens of Casa Grande matched that of Hettie Pierce. It had suffered a blow that would need a heap of soul-searching to recover.

Soon after leaving the town, the three men passed through a stand of organ pipe cacti. These straight-backed green jackets looked like a rampant army at the charge, the red fruit giving them a bloodstained appearance. Marching up one rise and down the other side, the lofty desert stalwarts maintained an unremitting advance.

Thereafter, sagebrush and mesquite dominated the landscape.

Even though it was a bleak and arid terrain, the trail was easy to follow due to ruts made by the regular passage of wagons and stagecoaches. The only problem was the shortage of waterholes. Gleeson had made due provision with goatskins that hung down from the sides of the heavily laden burro. The hardy beast of burden trotted to the rear, its lead rein held by Chickweed Prieta.

Ahead, the surging ramparts of the Tortilla Mountains presented a barrier that could only be breached in a few places.

One of these was a deep ravine known as the Klondyke. Rhodes Peak, which towered over the whole range, stood out proudly. It gave the illusory image of being almost within calling distance. Yet it was still a full day's ride away. The mirage is another strange phenomenon that seeks to trick unwary travellers into believing they are close to water.

Such is the enigmatically charged aura of the desert landscape.

Chad Gleeson was fully aware that it could never be

taken for granted. Respect for the harsh environment was a prerequisite for survival.

His two companions were no less wary of challenging the sudden changes that befall a man. Squirrel-Tooth Jones had once been stuck for three days in a violent sandstorm that had suddenly blown up while he was crossing the Sonora Desert east of Tucson. Forced to hunker down behind his horse, he lived on hard tack and beef jerky washed down by sips of tepid water.

The storm finally passed over, but not before he was forced to dig his way out of a deep drift. Unfortunately, his mount had suffocated under the thick mantle. Its mouth and nose were completely choked up by the noxious sand. Lady Luck, however, was smiling on Jones on that occasion. He was only a day's walk from Oracle Springs. Even so, the young cowboy was forced to take cover on three occasions when wandering bands of Mescalero Apaches were sighted.

On their present crossing of the desert, the eagle eyes of the three men spotted no Indian presence. Nonetheless, they entered the narrow confines of the Klondyke with trepidation, and rifles gripped firmly in their sweating hands.

'Keep your eyes peeled, boys,' Gleeson warned his associates. 'There is a band of renegades somewhere in these mountains led by that red devil Maranacas. I received a letter only the other day from the commanding officer at Fort Thomas.'

Buzzards wheeled overhead, circling ominously in

the hope of an easy meal. They were to be disappointed.

The tortuous trail, twisting through the bleak fastness of the Tortillas like a slithering sidewinder, took longer than expected. As a result, they were forced to spend a cheerless night hemmed in by the menacing turrets of rock.

Unlike his two buddies, Seven-Up passed an undisturbed night. Knowing that the notorious Maranacas was in the area, Jones and Prieta were more skittish than a pair of Mexican jumping beans. To them, every sound made by the creatures inhabiting the ravine was the stealthy approach of an Apache buck. They were more than ready for the false dawn to herald the start of a new day.

The nervous twitching of the two recruits amused Gleeson, although he hoped they would have more backbone when it came to challenging Dutch Henry and his gang. Judging by their recent antics, he was beginning to doubt the wisdom of hiring them. Nothing he could do about that now except trust those hoglegs strapped to their hips were not merely to impress the girls at the Saturday hoedowns.

It was around noon when the three riders entered Jacaranda.

The town was situated on the west bank of the San Pedro River. This spot was the narrowest place suitable for crossing within two days ride up or down stream. Enterprising pioneers had soon recognized it as a prime location for trading. And once a permanent wooden bridge had replaced the original ferry crossing, the town rapidly prospered.

Gleeson wasted no time in idle curiosity. He homed in to the source of any potential recruits for his posse.

The Lotus Eater saloon was like a hundred others of its kind throughout the western territories. A long mahogany bar stuck against one wall with tables and chairs dotted about. The gambling section was at the rear.

In the far left corner stood a battered upright piano on a tiny raised stage. When the three men entered the saloon, they were met by the merry jingle of a popular ditty. The player was enthusiastic if somewhat out of tune.

As it was the middle of the day, the place was rather quiet. That would no doubt alter as men finished work and congregated for some well-earned relaxation. The smell of the place made his nose wrinkle. A heady aroma of stale beer and tobacco smoke mingled with that of unwashed bodies.

Before making enquiries about potential recruits for the posse, they all needed a drink to wash the trail dust from their dry throats. Gleeson sidled up to the bar and ordered three beers.

'And make them cold, bartender,' added Chickweed Prieta, licking his desiccated lips in anticipation. He and Squirrel-Tooth were well used to such dives. 'My throat's rougher than a coyote's ass.'

His buddy howled with laughter.

The barman merely glowered at the young punks. 'You want ice, mister? There's plenty on the mountain tops. We don't have a cellar for that fancy stuff down here on the plains.' He hurried on after noting the tin star pinned to the older man's brown leather vest. 'You guys here on business?' The enquiry was delivered with nonchalant ease to conceal the bartender's innate curiosity.

Three foaming pots slid across the greasy counter. They were grabbed and knocked back, the amber liquid barely touching the sides. Refills were instantly called for. Warm or cold, the beer tasted like nectar.

Only when they paused for breath halfway through these did the lawman deign to enlighten the nosey 'keep and the rest of the Lotus Easter's clientele.

He turned round, resting his elbows on the bar, and surveyed the room. A lawman always attracted interest, usually of the suspicious variety. Nobody spoke.

'I'm Chad Gleeson, the sheriff of Pima County. My office is in Casa Grande,' he announced, peering round the room. 'Any of you fellas want to earn some easy dough?' The offer was accompanied by a smile more akin to that of a crafty fox.

'What's the catch?' called out a sceptical voice from the shadows.

'No catch,' replied Gleeson in a glib Seven-Up spiel while spreading his arms wide. 'All I need are a few bold characters to help me out. And you'll draw deputy sheriff's pay during your employment.'

'So what do we have to do?' enquired another punter who was rather more positive. Wearing a badge was a prestigious step up the slippery ladder of achievement for many of these jaspers.

Gleeson coughed before replying. This was going to

be the tough bit.

'I am after bringing in the Vandyke gang,' he said in a rather restrained voice. 'As you may know, they are wanted for armed robbery and rustling in New Mexico as well as here in Arizona. Well, now we can add murder and kidnapping to their list of crimes.'

Eyes bulged and mouths hung open on hearing this revelation. Once the grim truth of the lawman's request had sunk in, most of those present looked away. Conversations were resumed, cards dealt and drinks imbibed. The piano player resumed his much-needed practice.

'Well?' exclaimed Gleeson angrily. 'Isn't there one of you turkeys prepared to join my posse?'

Nobody responded to the vehement exhortation.

'Are all the jaspers in this town a bunch of weak-kneed spinsters?' The cutting barb was intended to stir some reaction. And it succeeded. A man pushed back his chair and stood up. Judging by his attire, he was a clerk.

'We ain't cowards, sheriff,' snapped the man. 'And neither are we dumb fools willing to sign our lives away. You're here to uphold the law. All I'm paid to do is tend store. Dutch Henry is ruthless and don't take no prisoners.'

The man had said his piece. Now he sat down, his stark comments eliciting murmurs of agreement amongst his associates.

Frustrated again, Chad turned back to the bar and sank the rest of his drink. An angry fist pummelled the counter.

While his back was turned, two men at the rear furtively left the saloon. They had both recognized the name of the tough sheriff and knew he was a dogged and determined law officer. But it had come as a shock to know that he and his two deputies were so close on their heels.

The search and pursuit of the gang had clearly already begun in earnest.

On first spotting the presence of a law officer in their midst, Trigger Wixx had nudged his snoozing partner into wakefulness.

Bonita was somewhat the worse for wear having consumed a full bottle of whiskey. He grunted, a lurid epithet spilling from between gritted teeth. It was when the sheriff introduced himself asking for recruits to join his posse that Slim Jim came fully awake. He quickly tried to shake off the numbing effects of the rotgut.

Wixx hunched his shoulders in an effort to remain incognito. Even though he had never set eyes on the sheriff before, it was the natural reaction of a man on the run. The fact that nobody had taken up the tin star's offer didn't matter. If'n Gleeson had come from his base at Casa Grande, Wixx knew that the trio were headed in the right direction for the Catalinas and Laughing Buzzard Canyon.

How had the canny lawdog managed to suss out the location of the gang's hideout? There was no time now for speculating on that mystery.

Outside on the street, Wixx insisted that the three men had to be stopped. Bonita was less enthusiastic. But he went along with his sidekick's plan.

'You go over there and hide behind those barrels,' Wixx urged his still bleary-eyed partner, pointing out the place of concealment. 'I'll hunker down behind those hay bales. That way we'll be able to catch the bastards in a crossfire when they come out of the saloon.'

Bonita gave a perfunctory nod and stumbled off the boardwalk. He pitched forward on to his face. Wixx spat out a muted curse at his drunken associate. Picking himself up, the stocky outlaw weaved a path over to the line of lamp oil barrels. Wixx scowled at the broad back. He prayed that the soused jigger would play his part.

Checking his revolver, Wixx slotted a sixth cartridge into the chamber that he always kept free to avoid accidents. The safety measure reminded him of the time that luck had deserted Latigo Chavez on one occasion before he ran foul of Dutch Henry in Hooker.

The greaser had shot himself in the leg during a pursuit by irate ranchers down in the border country close to Nogales. Following a perilous chase, they finally managed to cross into Mexico with most of the stolen herd intact. The only casualty had been Chavez. The jolting occasioned by the spirited dash had somehow cocked the hammer and discharged the gun.

It was only a flesh wound and he soon recovered. But the incident was a lesson learned by the rest of the gang. Leave the barrel chamber empty except when the need arose.

That need had now arrived.

He signalled to his partner across the street but received no acknowledgement. A few minutes passed before the doors of the Lotus Eater swung open. The rusty creak alerted Wixx. He thumbed back the hammer of his .44 Remington and took up a position affording him the best shot.

But in the still air, the sharp double click was a noise that Chad Gleeson had heard many times before. Like the lowing of cattle to a ranch hand, or the roll of dice to a gambler, discerning the ratchet of a sixgun from other sounds was a professional necessity for staying alive.

The sheriff's reaction was automatic. He threw himself to the ground while palming his own revolver.

'Hit the deck, boys,' he called out. 'We've gotten unwelcome company around.'

As if to confirm his observation, two shots rang out. They originated from the other side of the street. One bullet shattered a window in the saloon. The other took Prieta in the neck. Blood spurted from the fatal injury. The unlucky cowpoke threw up his arms and slid down the wall, a smear of blood trailing in his wake.

His pard was stunned into immobility by the sudden claim of the grim reaper.

'Take cover, kid,' rapped Gleeson, 'or you'll be joining your buddy.'

Jones did not need a second telling. He tried to hide behind one of the veranda uprights. It was not the safest place of concealment as he soon discovered when a lump of wood was removed inches from his head. The shot had once again come from across the street behind some barrels.

Ducking low, Jones replied with half his load. The

bushwhacker disappeared from view, giving the young cowpoke time to find a better place behind a wagon. His legs were partially exposed but at least his body was now concealed.

Wixx concentrated his fire power on the sheriff. The shining star offered the perfect target. And the sheriff was the more dangerous opponent. Bullets whistled over the sheriff's head. One removed his hat. Gleeson rolled off the boardwalk and into the street after noting the puffs of smoke curling above the hay bales. Winded by the heavy thud on hard ground, he gritted his teeth, shaking off the jar of pain.

This was no time for nursing injuries.

The assailant cursed aloud. His mark was now behind a row of horses standing at the hitching rail in front of the saloon. Frightened by the close eruption of gunfire, the animals were straining at their reins. A couple, less securely tethered than the rest, dragged free and stampeded up the street.

Wixx crawled out from cover, his gun pointed between the stamping legs of the remaining cayuses. But Gleeson was ready for him. Two well-placed shots struck the gunman in the head. He slumped to the ground out of the fray.

Still crouched down behind the barrels on the far side, Slim Jim continued to pour a stream of lead at the remaining deputy. The killing of Chickweed Prieta had been a propitious fluke of a shot.

In normal circumstances, his aim would have been much more accurate. He was an excellent marksman having won various competitions for his prowess with a rifle. His proudest possession was a 'One-in-a-Hundred Winchester Carbine', an achievement earned the previous summer in Dodge City, Kansas.

But on this May Day of 1878 in the Arizona town of Jacaranda, Slim Jim Bonita could not fully throw off the sluggish reaction of his body to the inflow of too much hard liquor. It had thrown his aim off.

Realizing that his buddy was down with two of the posse still far from beaten, he decided to quit while he still could.

After reloading from his shellbelt, Bonita emptied a full magazine at his adversaries. While they took cover, he ran off in the opposite direction. Even in his lethargic state of mind and carrying more than his share of weight, Bonita could shift when the occasion demanded. And that was surely now. Bullets buzzed and zipped around his head. It felt like the Devil was tickling his ass with a firebrand.

A block further down the street, Bonita had noticed a line of horses tied up on this side. His own chestnut was keeping company with the sorrel belonging to his dead partner outside the saloon. Bullets continued to pursue the outlaw, but luck was on his side.

He reached the line of mounts and leapt on to the first one. Hugging the bay's neck he swung away from the battle zone, presenting as small a target as possible. Spurs dug into the horse's flanks. The startled mare reared up on hind legs then charged off down the street eager to escape the terrifying outbreak of violence.

As the gunfire tailed off, people came flooding out

of the saloon and adjoining premises to enquire what the fracas was about.

At that moment all the two main participants were concerned about was their dead comrade. Squirrel-Tooth was inconsolable. Shoulders heaved in grief as he held the shattered body of his friend.

Gleeson was also distraught at losing half his posse. But he needed to channel the kid's anguish into a more constructive avenue. With every minute wasted on mournful outpourings, the bushwhacker was getting away.

'Somebody get the undertaker,' he announced to the crowd in general. 'We have to go after the killer. Him and his sidekick' – he pointed to the other dead body splayed out adjacent to the hay bales – 'must be members of the Vandyke Gang.'

A sharp intake of breath greeted this revelation.

Gleeson ignored the questions and comments. He gently drew his associate to his feet and addressed the cowpoke. The utterance was brisk and forthright. This was no time for gentle condolences.

'You want to catch up with the rat that did this, don't you, boy?' Jones gave a glum-faced nod. 'Your buddy has not given his life in vain. Now you have the chance to find the gang and get your revenge.' He held the young cowboy by the shoulders, fixing him with a gimlet eye. 'But we need to get on his trail pronto or he'll disappear. When our job is completed, we can come back this way and give Chickweed a proper burial. And I'll make darned sure he receives a fine send-off at the county's expense.'

The tough lawman eased the kid over to his horse. Squirrel-Tooth offered no resistance, allowing himself to be led away. Numbness suffused his whole being. The sudden outbreak of violence and its grim aftermath had left its mark on his soul.

SEVEN

BIRTH OF AN OUTLAW

Gleeson need not have worried. Trailing the panic-stricken Slim Jim Bonita was a piece of cake for a man of his prowess. The guy had given no thought to concealing his movements. So intent was he on getting back to Laughing Buzzard Canyon that all thoughts that he might be followed were forgotten.

The death of his partner had also left a chastening effect on the owl hooter's black soul. The notion that the renowned lawman would pick up his trail had not enter Bonita's soused brain when he skipped town in a galloping frenzy.

Feverishly, he berated his stolen horse, urging it to eat up the miles.

Gleeson and his associate followed at a more sedate pace. They stopped frequently to check the clues left by their quarry. Broken twigs, recent hoofprints, splashed rocks near to creek beds that had been crossed in a hurry. All these and more were like signposts pointing the way to Laughing Buzzard Canyon.

Near to one of the creeks, footprints denoted by the deep imprint of boot heels informed the ex-army scout that Bonita had been forced to walk his horse. Pushing a cayuse to the limit will quickly exhaust the animal.

Regular walking on long treks is essential for maintaining equine stamina. Even Jim Bonita would have been aware of this basic element of survival in the wilderness.

But the sheriff could not afford to be overly cautious. Once Dutch Henry was informed of the pursuit, and the grim fact that he was now a man down, the gang boss would not waste time in quitting his hideout.

Towards the end of the second day out from Jacaranda, the sheriff and his deputy reached the barrier of the Catalinas. A formidable bulwark that stretched east to west as far as the eye could see, this had to be where the Vandyke Gang were ensconced. The trail led down through narrow gullies to the base of the towering red sandstone cliffs.

And there, immediately ahead, was the narrow rift giving access to the inner sanctum. He drew to a halt behind some rocks.

'You stay here, Frank,' he said to his companion, 'while I check out the entrance. I need to find out if'n they've already left.'

He nudged his horse down the shallow grade, keeping a watchful eye on the heights above. Buzzards circled high in the azure firmament, eyeing the new-comer. Gleeson returned their arrogant scrutiny, hoping the angry cawing would not be heard by those he sought to apprehend.

There were plenty of hoofprints in the vicinity of the entrance to the Laughing Buzzard. But only one set were of recent origin, judging by their clearer depiction in the sand. And they were heading into the canyon. The edges of the older prints were less defined, indicating that nobody had come out lately.

He breathed out a sigh of relief. They were in time.

Swinging his horse around, he cantered back to rejoin his associate.

'Looks like they are still in there,' he murmured, once again scanning the arid terrain to ensure they were still alone. 'The killer is the only rider who has passed through the canyon. There's been no other movement in or out for at least two days.'

'What happens now then, sheriff?' Jones queried nervously, his squirrel teeth all the more prominent. 'We can't take on the whole gang single-handed.'

Gleeson sensed his partner's trepidation. He rolled a couple of stogies, lit them and handed one to Jones.

'Don't worry,' he said, laying a hand on the young cowpoke's shoulder to dispel his concern. 'I may be a hard-nosed bastard when it comes to dealing with brash kids . . .' Jones's face reddened. 'But I know when extra help is needed.'

Gleeson then went on to outline his plan.

'We still have a couple of hours left before dark.' He wandered over to the burro and dug out enough

73

supplies for a night's camp in the open. 'All being well, you should reach Fort Apache by this time tomorrow. Ask for Ellis Dudley. Tell him that I sent you. We go back aways. He and I were junior officers together in the War. Once he knows that we're on the trail of the skunks who killed his comrades, there ain't no doubting that he'll want to help catch them.'

'What happens if'n the gang leave the canyon before we get back here?' asked Jones, mounting up.

'I'll keep track of them from a distance and leave clear signs for you to follow. Now you best get going.'

The cowpoke hesitated. He needed to say something else.

'Guess I've grown up these last few days, sheriff.' He gripped his hat tightly, head bowed. 'Me and Chickweed were dumb asses doing what we did in Casa Grande. So I want to apologize for it on his behalf.'

Chad smiled and held out his hand. 'He didn't deserve to die like that and I'll make durned sure that your buddy gets justice.' They shook hands. Then Gleeson slapped the cowboy's horse on the rump.

He watched it disappear over the first rise then settled down to keep watch. It would have to be a dry camp. No way could he jeopardize revealing his presence. As dark shadows settled over the wild landscape, the sheriff withdrew the Wanted poster of Dutch Henry Vandyke and studied it closely. He wanted that face etched on to his mind while he slept.

'So what makes a skunk like you take to the owl hooter trail?' he muttered to himself while chewing on a stick of beef jerky.

If the Dutch immigrant had asked himself the same question, there would have been no need for thoughtful speculation. He knew exactly why he was now one of the most notorious outlaws of his generation.

It had all started when his parents occupied open land on the flat plains of Kansas.

Planting and harvesting crops on a small dirt farm was tough, back-breaking work. But young Henry had enjoyed the physical labour of farming. It fed the family and provided a little extra dough to acquire the necessities that could only be store-bought. In addition he had done his bit by supplementing the meagre diet with rabbits and deer shot with his Sharps rifle.

Life continued apace and the Vandykes made a reasonable living for themselves selling the crops harvested to merchants in the town of Wichita. And so it would have continued. Being immigrants, the civil war that tore the country apart had passed them by.

It was during the peace that followed when things went disastrously wrong.

Henry was making his monthly visit to Wichita to pick up the list of household provisions prepared by his mother. His return later in the day was to change the entire course of his life from thereon.

All appeared as normal as he drove the wagon into the yard fronting the basic homestead constructed of sods cut from the never-ending grass plain.

Smoke dribbled from the iron stovepipe poking through the new roof. The old sod one had been replaced a month before. As early as possible, Otto Vandyke had forked out for shingles. Sods attracted varmints and snakes in addition to being dirty and prone to leaking.

But where were his parents?

He called out. 'Ma! Pa! You guys in there?'

But there was no reply. Perhaps his father was out in the fields harvesting the crop of melons that grew so well hereabouts.

Another call went unanswered. A flicker of trepidation scurried down the young Dutchman's spine. He sensed that all was not right. Drawing his revolver, Henry stepped down off the wagon. Another wary look panned across the vicinity of the homestead. Only the squawking of a few hens disturbed the edgy silence. Gingerly, Henry approached the open door of the house. It swung in the breeze, squealing ominously on rusted hinges.

Pushing open the door he entered the soddy. His eyes took some moments in adjusting to the gloomy interior. Then he saw them, splayed out on the floor, blood dark and glutinous eking from the bullet wounds. A cry akin to that from a stricken animal rattled in his throat. Henry just stood there, glued to the spot. The traumatic sight had shut his brain down.

It was Blue, their Irish wolfhound, barking outside that jerked him back to the awful situation he now faced.

Who could have carried out such a brutal slaying? And why? Then he recalled an incident of the previous week. Three men had arrived offering to buy the land off his father. Dressed in store-bought suits they were clearly businessmen. The guy in charge introduced himself as Charlie Swiftnick from Missouri.

'As agent for the Kansas Freehold Company,' Swiftnick had announced in a cheerful tone. 'I have been authorized by my employers to offer you a fair price for this land, Mr Vandyke. The company are intending to develop it for the benefit of the territory. So you will be helping your fellow Americans by showing the community spirit that the government wishes to re-establish following the dire conflict of the last four years.'

Following this well-prepared speech, the man doffed his hat. Swiftnick was all charm and stuffed full of obsequious toadying. Compliments flowed thick and fast.

He even included Henry's mother by admiring her smart appearance. The new check dress she was wearing was a recent birthday present from her husband. Gretel Vandyke blushed, clearly smitten by such unaccustomed flattery.

'It is a good offer,' Swiftnick concluded, handing over a contract for the homesteader's appraisal. 'All you have to do is sign on the dotted line, and the money will be handed over. No more hard grafting for a pittance, just cold hard cash in your pockets to go wherever you choose. Your neighbours have already agreed to our proposal. You are my last call of the day.'

The man smiled. It emerged as a warped curl of the lip lacking any depth of sincerity. Otto did not even look at the document. He puffed out his chest and squared his broad shoulders. The amount offered was miserly. Not that he had any desire to sell up. This was his land. A free tract granted by the government, filed and registered with the local homesteading agency.

Neither was he swayed by the oily charm of the representative. He knew exactly why they were after his land. Others had come before with the same scheme in mind.

They were acting for large meat-processing enterprises from Chicago who wanted land to build cattle pens. Large herds were beginning to come up the trails from Texas. And with the burgeoning population back east craving beef and lots of it, dollars by the million were up for grabs.

But it all depended on acquiring the land to house the cattle herds while sales negotiations were completed. Only then could the railroad trucks be filled and despatched to their hungry destinations.

Many had indeed sold up, lured by the heady sales pitch and the flash of greenbacks. Others, like Otto Vandyke, were not so easily swayed by the paltry offers and flashy sales pitch.

'You can keep your offer, Mr, and your weasel words.' His response to the turkey's proposition was blunt and unequivocal. The older man had come across carpetbaggers before. They were sly chisellers seeking to make easy money by cheating law-abiding folks. 'I ain't selling to nobody. I know your kind. All you are after is making a fast buck at our expense.'

The charlatans were abruptly despatched with a flea in their ears.

The leader of the shifty trio had been none too pleased with the brusque refusal of his offer. Swiftnick had not said anything, but the black look aimed at Otto

78

Vandyke hinted that this was not the end of the matter. But the threatening glower was disregarded. These odious varmints had been sent on their way, so that was the end of the matter.

The cartpetbaggers were quickly forgotten. Until now.

Throwing off the shocking trauma that threatened to overwhelm him, Henry gulped air into his tight chest to bring his pounding heart under control. He knew that this bestial attack could only have happened in the last few hours. Unlike the more legitimate agents, Charlie Swiftnick and his cronies were not prepared to take no for an answer.

They had returned while he was away from the farm and exacted a brutal revenge.

The killers must have been waiting until he left the farm that morning which meant they were more than likely still in the area. Even now they could be in Wichita. He needed to get there pronto.

Henry Vandyke had vengeance in his heart as he spurred his horse back to town. He was not about to allow this heinous crime to go unpunished.

Common sense suggested that he inform the law and let them take charge. But Otto Vandyke had never placed much faith in the official avenues for seeking justice. That was the reason he had left Holland to seek his fortune in the New World. On that occasion it had been due to religious persecution.

Thereafter, he had encouraged his son to bear arms, teaching the youngster how to use them effectively.

'A man should be able to take care of his family,' was

the sound advice delivered in the gravelly accent of his homeland. 'He should not have to worry about the repercussions of taking the law into his own hands should the need arise.'

Those words had not done his father any favours. But Henry was determined that he would carry them out with vigour and decisive action to exact the full measure of justice in his own way. He gripped the butt of his .36 Navy Colt tightly. A bleak expression of steely resolve said it all. He was now after hunting human varmints rather than meat for the stewpot.

But first there was the distressing task of burying his parents next to the grave of their daughter who had died of consumption the previous year.

One of the first things Henry had done following the burial was to check the oak chest kept beneath his parents' bed. Anger soured his handsome face when he discovered it had been rifled and the land registry document stolen. No doubt by now it had been burned to destroy all evidence of ownership. Without that, Henry had no claim to the land.

Bidding farewell to the old homestead, he wondered if he would ever see it again. There was no telling how the implementation of his vow of reprisal would pan out.

Blue trotted at his heels as Henry Vandyke swung his horse north in the direction of Wichita. His face was grimly set, his gun hand itching to pull the trigger.

Once he reached the booming cattle town, Henry made straight for the first saloon on Butler Street. The Flat Iron was one of many such drinking dens catering to the summer arrival of cowboys fresh off the trail and seeking a good time.

'Has a guy called Charlie Swiftnick been in here?' he asked the bartender without any preamble. The man saw the look of fiery anger glittering in the youngster's fixed regard.

'I don't know anybody by that name,' he replied. Then, turning to some other drinkers, he said, 'Any of you fellas know a Charlie Swiftnick?' Nobody responded. 'This guy done something to upset you, mister?' the barman asked tentatively.

This was Henry's first visit to a saloon. Being of a strong religious persuasion, his parents had always discouraged the imbibing of alcohol.

'You could say,' was the brusque response. But Henry did not enlighten them. He merely nodded then walked out, stamping up the street to the next saloon. This happened in three other establishments with no luck. Henry was beginning to have doubts whether the guy had indeed come to Wichita.

It was when he came to enter the Cattle Queen that his luck changed.

Sitting at a table bold as brass, and playing poker as if nothing untoward had happened, was the murdering skunk himself. He appeared to be alone. Although Swiftnick's back was to him, there was no mistaking that arrogant posture and the natty duds. All of the rat's attention was focused on the game of chance.

Henry seethed at the guy's effrontery, his disdainful nerve. Any normal thief would have skipped the territory and waited for the hue and cry to die down before making a claim to the land he had killed to obtain.

Maybe he figured to have got away with the heinous crime and could afford to hang around.

Or perhaps he just didn't give a tinker's cuss.

All these thoughts washed over the avenger's head. All he knew or cared about was that the killer of his parents was about to pay for his crime. The law was irrelevant. Henry Vandyke would exact his own form of justice.

The kid stopped some six feet from the table. His whole body was trembling with a blend of hate and nervous apprehension.

Others in the vicinity sensed the newcomer's anger and that an eruption was about to occur. They moved away out of the line of fire. Henry flexed the fingers of his gun hand. Forcing himself to remain calm, he sucked in a deep breath.

'On your feet, Swiftnick!' The blunt order emerged as a grating snarl. The measured delivery faltered. His tremulous voice cracked with emotion as he continued. 'You murdered my folks because they wouldn't sell up. Then you and your bunch of scum stole their land deed. Now you're gone pay for it, you dirty coward. An eye for an eye, it says in the good book. And I am a God-fearing avenger here to carry out the Lord's bidding.'

It was a long speech for a young man who was far more comfortable with a ploughshare and scythe than words. Nothing like it had previously been delivered at one time in his whole life.

The killer's back stiffened. All play at the table ceased. Nobody else moved.

Slowly, Swiftnick pushed back his chair and stood up,

still keeping his back to his nemesis. Then, living up to his name, the killer swung on his boot heels, a small derringer clutched in his right hand. It had been tucked up his sleeve. A hidden means of defence for just such a crisis as he now faced.

The gun spat flame from the single barrel. Henry saw the sneaky manoeuvre just in time. He leaned to one side. But a searing pain shot through his left arm. Seeing that he had missed his mark, the killer panicked and threw the empty pistol at his opponent. Henry ducked. It sailed over his head and smashed a window.

Without any further delay, he drew his own weapon and fired. Henry's shot was spot on target. It punched Swiftnick back. Arms flailing wildly, the carpetbagger's legs crumpled, blood rapidly spreading across his chest. A second bullet finished the job. The dead body slammed down on to the card table, scattering money and chips across the floor.

Before the smoke had a chance to disperse, a voice cut through the rising babble from the other patrons of the Cattle Queen.

'Drop that gun, Mr, you're under arrest!'

But Henry Vandyke's blood was up. Without thinking he swung round and drilled another two shots at the man standing behind him. Only when the man dropped the shotgun clasped to his chest did the Dutchman see the tin star pinned to his vest. Marshal Cole Gleeson collapsed amid gasps of shock.

The lawman was a popular figure in Wichita. Even though the wild cattle town advertised itself as '*a place where anything goes*', he was respected by folks from both sides of the tracks. Allowing the itinerant cowboy population to enjoy itself while maintaining control of their boisterous antics was a tightrope walk he had managed with aplomb.

An angry murmuring broke out. The crowd were restive. Henry knew he had to be decisive to avoid the brusque retaliation of vigilante law. He had no doubts that should he be apprehended, a neck-tie party would be the inevitable result.

He fired another shot at the ceiling. It did the trick. The surging throng was halted in its tracks.

'Anyone moves and he'll get more of the same,' snapped the frightened youngster, waving his pistol around.

He lamented gunning down the lawman. Assuming the challenge had come from one of Swiftnick's gang, he had acted on instinct. But it was done now. Nothing would bring the guy back.

As for the shooting of Charlie Swiftnick, there were no regrets.

Henry's priority now, however, was to escape with his skin intact. He backed towards the door of the saloon.

The atmosphere in the Cattle Queen was thick with menace. All it needed was for one reckless dude to precipitate a stampede in his direction. A lone gunman with only one bullet remaining stood no chance against an entire saloon.

Some hero over to his right figured that he was the man. The guy reached for his gun. The movement caught Henry's attention. He immediately despatched his final slug at the wayward chancer. A scream cut through the tense silence. But it had the effect of post-poning any further attempt to capture the miscreant.

Henry took full advantage of the lull by exiting the saloon. His horse was close by. Leaping into the saddle, he threw the empty pistol through the window and gal-loped off down the street.

That was Dutch Henry Vandyke's introduction to a life of lawless endeavour. The killing of Charlie Swiftnick was only the beginning. He made it his busi-ness to hunt down and eradicate the others who had been party to the murder of his parents. After that there was no turning back.

As time passed he gathered a band of roughnecks together which had since caused mayhem across the western territories.

EIGHT

RED FOR DANGER

Chad Gleeson had learned about the death of his elder brother while working as a guard for the Union Pacific Railroad Company. He had come west in search of the killer. By accepting the role of deputy sheriff, he had hoped to legitimize his hunt for Henry Vandyke. This was the closest he had come in the last few years to catching up with Cole's murderer.

He was unaware of the circumstances that had pitched the Dutch outlaw into a life of crime. Nor did he care. All that concerned Seven-Up Gleeson was obtaining justice for the shooting-down of his kin.

The sun had risen over the Catalina Mountains when he was jerked awake. Stomping hoofs and the jingle of harness tack indicated that a body of horsemen was on the move. The noise echoed up from the valley below where he was concealed. Instantly alert, the sheriff scuttled over to the lip of the rocky shelf to confirm his suspicions.

And there in the lead was his nemesis. Chad gritted his teeth, grinding them in fury. This was the first time he had set eyes on the man who had killed his brother.

At that distance it was impossible to pick out any features. But he was within rifle range. Chad stuck the .44 Whitney-Burgess rifle to his shoulder and sighted along the hexagonal barrel. His finger tightened on the trigger. All it would take was a single squeeze and he would have his revenge.

Then he noticed the long auburn tresses just behind the gang leader. If'n he took out Dutch Henry, what would happen to the woman? There was still the rest of the gang to consider. Not to mention the gold bullion they were carrying in those heavy saddle-packs.

No! He needed to rein in that impatient streak that both the Gleeson brothers had inherited from their father. Chad counted off the nine other members of the group. Including Vandyke, that made ten altogether.

Seven was the total number reported by Bull Ferris after the robbery, which included two bogus passengers; although the sheriff could distinctly recall that the Wanted dodger said there were nine outlaws in the gang. He unfolded the poster to check. And there it was. Vandyke must have recruited some more critters since the robbery. This was going to be a much tougher proposition than he had figured.

At least the gang was one down. The body of Trigger Wixx had been left behind in Jacaranda.

Gleeson sombrely stuck the poster back in his pocket and proceeded to saddle up his horse. Allowing plenty of time for the gang to get on their way, he then made a careful descent to ground level and the entrance to Laughing Buzzard Canyon.

Here he dismounted and extracted a red shirt from his pack. A sigh of regret followed as he tore the shirt into strips. The snazzy item had been spotted in a mail-order catalogue. It had only arrived the previous week and the purchaser had not even tried it on yet.

But the bright colour made the perfect trail marker for Frank Jones and the army troopers to follow. He tied a piece to the branch of a Joshua tree, ensuring it was in a prominent position. Others would be left at strategic locations. Should the time come when he ran out of material . . . well, that would have to be faced later.

Gleeson tried to put himself into the mind of Dutch Henry.

The guy was likely heading south for the Mexican border. That was the best place to exchange gold bullion for hard currency. And with the revolutionaries causing trouble, he would have no trouble getting a good exchange rate. In a place like Mexico, gold was a far more valuable commodity than paper money.

So which way would he head?

The lawman gave this a great deal of consideration as he trailed the gang. Vandyke would not want to waste time. So the most direct course seemed the likely option.

He would want to avoid the major settlements of

Tucson, Coronado and Nogales. That intimated the gang would cross the Mescal Mountains by way of Jerusalem Pass, thereafter taking the San Philipe Valley to Benson. From there it was a straight trek south across Dragoon Flats to Tombstone.

An old buddy of the sheriff's called Wyatt Earp had recently moved to the booming silver-mining town. Vandyke would not want to linger there. Being so close to the border, his aim would be to continue south through the rolling desert country, crossing into Mexico somewhere south of Bisbee.

With that in mind, Gleeson felt confident of being able to trail the gang without the need to keep them in view all the time.

By maintaining a low profile, he was able to follow the clear trail left by the passage of numerous horses. On these sections, there was no need to leave a marker. It was in the traversing of watercourses and rocky arenas, where the visible trail disappeared, that help for the pursuers was most essential. That was also when he needed to speed up to make eye contact with his quarry.

On the third day out, he figured the army patrol under the command of Ellis Dudley ought to catch him up around noon of the following day.

That was always assuming Squirrel-Tooth Jones had managed to persuade the cavalry officer that he was on the level. The young cowhand did not exactly portray an aura of confidence. Gleeson was glad that he had given the kid his lucky seven medallion. The totem should be enough to convince the army man that the young cowpoke had been sent by his old comrade-in-arms. Ellis was well aware of his friend's penchant for the game of Seven-Up.

It was while Gleeson was looking for a secure place to bed down for the night that he sensed that all was not right. He scratched the old war wound on his neck. It always acted up when danger lurked nearby. As a shadow trailing the Vandyke Gang, he now harboured an unpleasant notion that he himself was being tracked.

If'n it was Jones with the soldier boys, they had got here much earlier than expected. The innate caution essential for survival at the sharp end of the legal profession now stepped in. Nothing could ever be taken for granted.

Two or three times a day, he had thus far made a habit of stopping to study his backtrail. It was on the last occasion that he had spotted the telltale signs of pursuit. A flock of cactus wrens had suddenly launched themselves skywards. It looked as if they had been disturbed. Perhaps a wild animal had frightened them. Or maybe it was something infinitely more sinister, like a human interloper.

As the shadows lengthened, Gleeson concealed himself behind some rocks where he could watch the trail. He hung around there for a half-hour. Then he saw him, a lone rider who was clearly following in his wake.

The lawman scowled. It sure wasn't Jones. Not wearing a wide Mexican sombrero. The mysterious stalker could easily have followed the more well-defined trail left by Vandyke and his men. But he must have picked up on the red shirt markers.

The lawman scratched his neck again. Who was the guy? A filament of deductive reasoning inherent in all seasoned lawmen began to churn away inside his head. The presence of a tail could mean only one thing.

This guy was the missing member of the gang. He must have been elsewhere when his sidekicks had departed from the Laughing Buzzard. Knowing the direction the gang was headed, the outlaw would have had no problem in catching them up. But he had seen the markers and put two and two together, reaching the obvious conclusion that someone else had sussed out their plans.

So what to do about the unknown tracker?

Making camp in a clearing with rocks on three sides, Chad was able to make a fire for the first time in three days, knowing it would only be spotted by the man following him. The idea was to make the guy assume his quarry was unaware that he was being followed. Over-confidence is apt to lower a man's guard. The lawman was also in no doubt that his pursuer would wait until he was sound asleep before attacking.

Following a hot meal, Chad stoked up the fire. Then he placed his gear beneath a blanket. With his hat resting at the top end on his saddle, the pretence was complete. Even from close up, the effect was undeniably that of a slumbering man. Gleeson was well satisfied with his deception.

Secreting himself behind a boulder, he settled down to wait.

It was another hour before a shadow appeared at the entrance to the clearing.

The black silhouette paused. Ensuring that his victim was indeed in the land of Nod, the killer then crept across the open sward. Silently, Gleeson emerged from where he had been hiding and cat-footed up behind the unsuspecting killer. The man had a large bowie knife clutched in his right hand. The lawman waited until he bent over the dark form beside the flickering embers of the fire.

The deadly blade lifted ready to deliver the *coup de grace.*

That was all the proof Chad needed that this skunk's avowed intention was to kill him. Until that moment, he might just have been a curious traveller seeking refreshment and warmth. The lawman raised the tomahawk he always favoured as a throwing weapon. The last thing he needed was any gunplay to warn Vandyke that he was being pursued.

But the guy must have sensed that he was being suckered. Or was it the lawman's heavy breathing that had alerted him? This was no time to consider the whys and wherefores. Seven-Up's life was at stake. The predator swung round to see his intended victim no more than ten feet away.

The dancing flames from the fire reflected off the metal star pinned to Gleeson's vest. Without a second's thought, the Mexican flicked his knife at the skulking lawdog. Inevitably, the attempted retaliation was hurried. And in the merky shadows of darkness, the blade merely sliced through Chad's shirt. It did, however, draw blood, the abrupt stab of pain extracting a taut grimace.

The lawman stumbled to the ground, dropping the tomahawk. This gave his attacker time to haul out a Manhattan .31 pistol. Gleeson knew that his stratagem was falling apart. A miracle was needed if he were to come out of this alive.

Thankfully Lady Luck now came to his rescue. A groping hand scraped against a stone. Without a second's thought, he grabbed the unexpected weapon and hurled it at the rising gun arm.

It was a panic-stricken lunge, but accurate enough to strike the varmint on the head. The blow stunned the Mexican, making the gun fall from his hand.

So far no words had been uttered by either protagonist. Rasping grunts and heavy breathing testified to the concentration of each battler to outwit his adversary. The advantage now fell to Gleeson, who grabbed up the fallen tomahawk. Balancing on his feet he hurled the weapon overhand at the silhouette etched black against the orange tongues of flame, its shiny blade glinting in the firelight.

The bushwhacker never saw the harbinger of death winging his way. And it was a good throw. The sharp-pointed axe buried itself deep in the man's chest. A whoosh of air was expelled from the open mouth as he staggered back. A weak hand tried desperately to drag the blade out of his ribcage. But it was stuck fast.

Already, the grim reaper was knocking on the door, and his call was emphatic. There would be no reprieve for Manuel Ramirez. He had only been with the gang a month, having replaced his unlucky countryman following the death of Chavez. Now it was his turn to stoke up the fires of hell.

As Ramirez slumped to the ground, Gleeson breathed deep, his heart pumping like a steam engine. That had been a close thing. On this occasion he had been extremely fortunate. Next time the gods might not smile on him so graciously.

A quick search of the Mexican's pockets revealed some American dollars which Gleeson pocketed – the spoils of war. He also found a grainy photograph of a pretty young woman. On the back was a scrawled message which read: *Conchita, mi periquito*. For a brief instant Gleeson felt a sense of regret at the Mexican outlaw's passing. Everyone has a past, a lovebird such as this to miss them.

The feeling passed quickly. It had been him or me, the lawman surmised. And Manuel Ramirez had lost. Lugging the heavy body over to some rocks, he dumped it out of sight where the smell would not disturb him or his horse.

Then he settled down for the night.

Another day and a half went by before the telltale signs of a large body of riders was spotted to the rear. Surely this had to be Jones and the troopers. Once again, Chad made certain of their identity before revealing himself.

'Glad to see you again, lieutenant,' the officer in charge greeted his old associate with a wide grin. 'Must be all of ten years since our paths crossed. You ain't changed a bit.'

Chad tapped his chest. 'I'm a sheriff these days, Ellis. Glad to see you've moved up in the world as well. A full-blown major now, eh?' He chuckled. 'There's enough scrambled egg on that uniform to feed a regiment.'

The accompanying troopers couldn't resist a sly grin between themselves. Major Dudley joined in the banter. He was a well-respected officer amongst the men he had brought along. All of them had volunteered for this mission once they were appraised of its significance.

After exchanging a few words and catching up on each other's adventures since their parting of the ways, Chad brought the army man up to date with the current situation as it now stood. Dudley's face assumed a sombre mien.

The officer who had been killed in the Tonto Valley was from his own company.

Gleeson led his old colleague over to where he had concealed the corpse of the bushwhacker. The officer called for one of his men to join them.

'Have you seen this critter before, sergeant?' he asked a burly, red-headed trooper.

Brad Driscoll's dark eyes opened wide as he pointed a startled finger at the Mexican. 'This varmint was plying my men with drink in the saloon at the fort, sir,' he exclaimed. Then he called out to a small guy with a prominent nose and close-set, beady eyes. 'Hey, Riley, over here pronto!'

Known as Mouse for obvious reasons, Riley hurried over to join them.

'Is this the guy who was trying to get the boys to

reveal details of the regiment's plan to investigate the lost patrol?'

Private Mouse Riley sniffed as he peered down at the dead Mexican.

'Sure looks like him, sergeant,' he confirmed, aiming a contemptuous gob of spittle at the blood-stained corpse. 'The other guys were happy to down the liquor he was handing out. But I was suspicious. Why was a greaser interested in this particular incident?' He shrugged. 'Then he left the saloon. And I didn't give it much thought after that.' The little trooper's thin lips tightened. 'Now I know what his game was.'

Riley's probing gaze then shifted to the doughty sheriff.

'Looks like he upset somebody else and paid a heavy price.'

'The guy was following me,' Gleeson replied. 'So I set a trap for him. Unfortunately I didn't manage to learn what he was up to. But my figuring is that he is a member of the Vandyke Gang who killed that missing patrol. Dutch Henry, the leader, must have sent him to the fort to suss out the army's plans. Some of your guys must have let slip that you were headed this way.'

'It sure is a good job that he didn't get through.' The officer shook his head, adding gravely, 'If'n he had, there ain't no doubting that we would have ridden into a trap. This gang is a dangerous menace and must be brought to justice before any more innocent people are killed.'

All the troopers, including Major Dudley, now looked to the lawman for his leadership in their quest to hunt down Dutch Henry and his gang. Chad Gleeson had been raised to a new level of respect in their critical eyes. That was no mean feat. Military personnel of all ranks seldom held civilian aides in great respect unless exceptional circumstances prevailed.

Davy Crockett, Kit Carson and Jedediah Smith were three such luminaries. To that august body had been added Seven-Up Chadwick Gleeson – at least in the eyes of this small band of bluecoats, not to mention Squirrel-Tooth Jones.

'So how do you plan to capture these skunks, Seven-Up?' asked Dudley.

Total responsibility for the mission had unwittingly been conferred into his hands. The lawman knew that much now rested on his broad shoulders. 'Our main task is to rescue the woman that Vandyke is holding,' he declared firmly. 'Once she is out of danger, then you boys can take it from there. But recovery of the gold bullion has to be a second priority.'

Dudley concurred with the lawman's sentiment. 'We can't plan any attacking strategy until we see what the combat terrain is like,' he said. 'And it's too late to do anything today. Mind if'n we join your camp?'

'There's coffee on the fire, help yourselves.' Chad indicated the blackened pot resting on a stone beside the smouldering embers of the fire. 'Although I ain't toting no fancy vittles.'

'We have enough grub for a solid meal,' the officer declared. 'Yancy is the best cook in the regiment. And he always makes sure we eat well on patrol.' He nodded for a portly trooper to unpack the necessary equipment. 'You recall that well known saying, don't you, Chad?'

'Remind me.'

'An army always marches on its stomach. Well, that's certainly true of Private Yancy.'

The other troopers chuckled as the hefty cook went about his task in a businesslike manner. The joshing was light-hearted. They were all eager and grateful to partake of Yancy's culinary expertise. It had been a long trek from Fort Apache. And they were tired and hungry.

NINE

RESCUE

It was two days later that the combined civilian/military assault team caught up with Vandyke and his crew of misfits. The western sky was a blaze of fire as the setting sun dipped below the Mescal Mountains. The gang had made camp at the head of a shallow wash. Just as Gleeson had surmised, Dutch Henry's intention was to negotiate a passage through the mountains afforded by Jerusalem Gap. Once he had reached the far side, an easy trek down the San Philipe Valley would follow.

The glow from a fire showed above the rim of the depression.

Gesturing silently, Gleeson indicated for Major Dudley to join him. Together they crept up to the edge and peered over. Vandyke was clearly not expecting trouble. He had not even posted a guard. His men were busy with the variety of chores that needed doing before they settled down for the night.

A picket line had been set up to one side.

Separate from the others, the woman was sitting alone on a log combing her hair. Gleeson sucked in his breath. That bone drummer had not lied. Even from this distance he could tell that she was no plain Jane. If nothing else, Dutch Henry certainly had good taste in women.

The gang leader called across to her in a starchy voice. His dialogue was indistinct but the meaning was obvious. Terminating her ablutions, Lucy Calendar sauntered over to the fire and began arranging the cooking pots. She had clearly been given the job of camp cook.

'We need to establish where the woman is going to bed down for the night,' he whispered to his associate. 'Then I can sneak down there and release her.'

'You sure that's wise, Chad?' cautioned his buddy. 'If'n you're spotted, we'll have lost the element of surprise.'

'I need to get her out of there while it's still dark,' Gleeson explained. 'Then you boys can do what you do best without her getting caught in a crossfire.'

'I catch your drift,' Dudley agreed. 'Will you need any help?'

Gleeson considered the suggestion. 'Reckon I'll take Squirrel-Tooth along. He can keep a watch on my back.'

'A night attack on their position is too hazardous,' advised the military man. 'Some of the gang could make good their escape under cover of darkness. As you know, it's always best to attack at dawn when you can see the lie of the land and your enemy is at his most vulnerable.'

Gleeson nodded. The tactics of military campaigns were beginning to come back to him. 'I'm rusty in that department. What have you in mind?'

'Once you have successfully rescued the woman, I'll divide the troop into two sections. Then we'll attack them using the classic pincer movement. I'll lead the left arm with Sergeant Driscoll taking the right.' He snapped his fingers as a past thought re-established itself in his mind. 'Remember the Nutcracker Operation we launched at Chancellorville?'

Gleeson's response was a broad grin. 'That sure was something,' he gushed, slapping his friend on the back. 'Them Johnny Rebs didn't know what had hit them.'

'We'll try the same stunt here on a miniature scale.'

Major Dudley turned round and signalled for Sergeant Driscoll to join them. Once the burly bluecoat had scrambled up the shallow grade, the officer informed him of their plans.

'Post a two-hour guard detail to watch the camp, sergeant,' he ordered in a decisive yet subdued tone of voice. 'Any movement down there, let me know immediately. We will be making our assault on the camp at first light. And it goes without saying that it will be a cold camp tonight. No fires.'

Driscoll snapped out a parade-ground salute. 'Yes, sir!' As the sergeant was about to retreat back down the slope to arrange things, the major licked a finger and stuck it into the air. One last order then followed.

'And no smoking!' Dudley fixed a pertinent eye on

to his sergeant. 'It's only a light breeze but the smell of tobacco smoke will give our position away.'

'Leave it to me, major.'

Dudley was confident that the solidly reliable non-com would ensure his orders were carried out to the letter.

It was in the early hours that a nudge from the guard just finishing the middle shift brought Gleeson instantly awake. 'According to the setting of the stars it's four o'clock, sheriff,' the man hissed. 'That was when I was told to waken you.'

Gleeson was impressed. A man who could tell the time by studying the heavens was to be commended.

'Much obliged, soldier. That's a rare skill you have there. What's your name?'

'Private Matt Hawkins, sir,' came the muted response. 'The boys call me Moonglow.'

'I can see why,' said Gleeson, pulling on his boots.

'My pa taught me all about navigating at night by the stars. He used to be a sailor. It's called astronomy.'

The sheriff checked his revolver and took a sip of water before returning to the matter uppermost in his mind. 'Has there been any movement in the outlaw camp during your watch, Moonglow?'

'No, sir,' replied the young trooper. 'And the hostage is still sleeping in the same position over by a clump of creosote bushes on the left. She hasn't moved since they bedded down for the night. And this bunch of turkeys are so darned cocky that they haven't even bothered to post a guard.'

Gleeson nodded his thanks. That was good news. It

would make his task all the easier. It also meant that Miss Calendar was on the outer edge of the camp separate from the rest. Vandyke appeared to be leaving her alone, at least for the time being. But Gleeson was not particularly reassured. He knew that most outlaws were volatile and unpredictable characters. So there was no telling what direction such an erratic mind would follow.

The sooner he got the woman out of Vandyke's odious clutches the better.

'You inform Major Dudley that me and my buddy are off to get the woman,' the sheriff instructed Trooper Hawkins. 'He knows what to do next.'

As the young soldier scuttled away, Gleeson edged back up to the crest of the knoll. Following on his heels was the eager young cowboy.

'What's the plan, sheriff?' he whispered.

A quick scan of the camp told him that all was as Hawkins had said. Most of the gang were clustered around the dying embers of the fire. Behind were the horses standing side by side secured by a picket line.

He could just make out the still form of the hostage over near the bushes.

He pointed her out to Jones. There was no sign of any other movement.

'You keep out of sight behind me,' he replied. 'Only cut loose with your hogleg if'n the balloon goes up, savvy?'

'Yes, sir!' the kid assured his associate.

Moving as silently as possible, they descended the slope, circling around to the left. Gun in hand and heart in mouth, Gleeson carefully picked a tenuous course across the uneven terrain. Any disturbance of rocks might easily warn the gang to the fact that they were not alone. Lucky for him, the moon was bright as a button in the clear night sky.

He knew that Ellis Dudley would now be moving his men into strategic positions around the edges of the camp. All he could do was pray that the gang would not be alerted before he had rescued the woman.

Keeping to the outer limit of the camp just beyond the flickering light cast by the fire, he crawled ever closer to his target. When the moment finally arrived to wake her up, he needed to ensure that she did not cry out.

An owl hooted away to the north. It was answered by the far-off howl of a coyote.

A hand reached out and hovered above the serene countenance. Gleeson hesitated, peering down at the innocent face. Frown lines, the result of her terrifying ordeal, were enhanced by streaks of trail dirt. But they did nothing to mar the woman's striking allure. Never had he set eyes on such a lovely creature. The tough lawman's heart melted. He wanted to stroke her smooth cheeks, set her mind at rest that she was now safe.

Then reality leapt to the fore, instigated by a movement near the picket line. A man had suddenly appeared from behind the horses. So Moonglow had been mistaken. A guard had been posted after all. The guy walked out into the open and made his way over to the fire.

104

Gleeson gave thanks to the innate caution he had exercised. Slowly and with infinite care he removed his hand and slid down into the shadows behind the girl.

So near yet so far.

The man poured himself a mug of coffee before returning to his post.

Gleeson cursed. This guy would need to be eliminated before he could rescue the woman. Slowly he circled around behind where the horses were picketed. His narrowed gaze tried to locate where the critter was positioned. But the guard had disappeared into the murk beyond the faint light from the camp fire. Another angry curse rumbled in the lawman's throat.

Then the stalker was given a stroke of luck as a match flared. Thereafter the red glow from a cigarette was like a homing beacon. The dark profile was leaning against a tree no more than twenty feet from where Gleeson was crouched. Holstering the revolver, he withdrew a knife from its sheath.

The cluster of palo verde trees afforded excellent cover as he crept silently towards his prey. No desert predator could have been stealthier. This was a hunt he could not afford to mess up.

Although he didn't realize it, Seven-Up was enacting a similar scenario as that in the Tonto Basin when Lieutenant Chadwick and his men were ambushed. The roles were now reversed. But would the result be the same?

In a brief moment he had sidled up behind the tree on the far side of which stood the guard. He sucked in a lungful of air, not daring to breathe lest the guy be alerted. Buckey Sontag was no more than an arm's length away. One thing Gleeson could not still was a drumming heart hammering at his ribcage. To him it sounded like a stampeding herd of buffalo.

The outlaw, however, remained motionless, completely oblivious to his presence.

Slurping at his coffee, Sontag puffed on his cigarette. At any moment he might shift his position away from the tree. Killing him then would become that much more difficult. It had to be done now.

Inching round the thick trunk of the lone cottonwood, he tossed a small pebble to the other side of the outlaw. A tiny chink of sound, it nonetheless drew the Sontag's head. Gleeson grabbed his one and only chance. A quick slash of the bowie knife and a broad scarf of red opened up around the outlaw's neck. Blood gushed from the fatal wound soaking his shirt front.

Gleeson clamped a hand over his gaping mouth to prevent any reflexive cry for help. The body shuddered as death claimed it. The lawman hung on grimly until the wracking torment had subsided. Then he carefully lowered the heavy body to the ground. Probing eyes darted across to the sleeping forms by the camp fire to make certain the rest of the gang had not been disturbed.

All remained still and quiet.

Backing off, Gleeson hustled back to where the woman was lying. The still form assured him that she also was totally unaware of the brutal exit of Buckey Sontag from this mortal coil. He looked across to where Jones was crouched. A brief wave of acknowledgement passed between them.

A soft glow in the east told him that dawn was fast approaching as he peered down at her. Willowy tresses, soft and graceful, framed a tranquil countenance that was mesmeric. Without any further delay, he clamped a hand over her mouth.

Instantly brought awake, her eyes gaped wide. Pure terror registered on the startled face. Her body stiffened with fear. A gentle yet insistently reassuring hush from her rescuer soon calmed the woman down.

'No need to be frightened, miss,' Gleeson whispered. 'I'm here to get you out this mess.' All the while his eyes were checking out the slumbering bodies round the fire. 'There is a patrol of soldiers over that knoll waiting for my signal to launch their attack. So we need to get out of here pronto. You understand me?'

The girl nodded her head as he removed his hand. Her mouth opened to speak, but Gleeson laid a finger on the pouting lips. His own were so very close. Even in this critical situation, he felt the urge to kiss her. But he resisted. This was neither the time nor the place for such heartfelt desires.

'Not now, miss. We need to go.'

He helped her up. Luckily she was still fully clothed. Edging her away from the immediate danger zone, there was still the problem of getting back to their own camp without disturbing the outlaws. With this in mind, he took a longer route back around the lower reaches of the hill where any slippages would not matter. All the while, Squirrel-Tooth kept a close watch on their backs.

Eventually, after negotiating various obstacles in the

form of tree roots, broken branches and boulders, the trio made it back to the camp. A trooper by the name of Sam Biglow had been left behind to meet the lawman and his liberated charge.

'Glad you made it back safely, sheriff,' he said in greeting. A crisp salute automatically followed. 'And you as well, miss.'

Lucy Calendar gave the trooper a tired wave. She slumped down totally drained, although elated that her torment had been concluded.

'Believe me, soldier,' sighed Gleeson, returning the acknowledgment as the tension drained from his tight frame, 'you ain't half as pleased as we are.'

'Major Dudley and the others should be in position by now, sir,' Private Biglow continued, while gathering his gear together. 'The major told me to report back once your mission had been successfully completed. You and your partner are to stay here and rest up, he said. It's our turn for some action now.'

TEN

. . . AND REVENGE!

The first the gang of outlaws knew that they were under attack was the raucous blast of a bugler announcing the charge. A thundering of hoofs shook the ground as the line of troopers hurtled down the slope. With sabres drawn, their curved blades pointing forward, the troupers added their own war cries to the guttural mêlée.

Major Dudley had elected to make his pincer assault from the western side of the camp so as to present less of a target. In contrast his foe would be silhouetted against the eastern skyline when they tried to retaliate. This was a conflict that was personal to the cavalry of Fort Apache.

Each of the men had known those who had been murdered in the Tonto Basin. So revenge was in their hearts. Any chivalric notion of taking prisoners was pushed to the back of their minds. Revenge is a potent emotion that ignores the common decencies associated with professional military discipline. Frontier justice could be swift and terminal. Vigilante law administered by unofficial drumhead courts was commonplace in remote outposts. In consequence, there would be no mercy shown on this day.

Whoops and bellowing roars ripped apart the early morning quietude as the troopers urged their mounts to the gallop. Eli Patch had been a popular man, always ready to lend a helping hand to those in trouble. His actions had more than once resulted in a spell in the guardhouse. All the others had friends who were now eager to avenge the patrol's heinous slaying by these cowardly brigands. Even the irritating grumbles of that layabout Jaybird would be missed.

And Lieutenant Chadwick had been under the personal supervision of Ellis Dudley. The young Westpointer had shown great potential that would now never be realized.

So the major was no less eager than his men to make things right in true frontier fashion. He looked on this attack as a miniature recreation of the war against the Sioux back in 1876. Luck had smiled on Captain Dudley that July day when he had been seconded to General Terry's rearguard division. Had he remained with the ill-fated George Armstrong Custer, his would have been a short-lived army career.

This was the first opportunity since the previous year's disaster for him to display his mettle. Clutching the banner of the 5th Cavalry's 3rd regiment of horse, he led his men into the fray.

'Don't let any of these varmints escape, men,' he hollered above the cacophony of the charge. 'This is for our murdered comrades.'

The gang were taken completely by surprise. Lumbering to their feet, addled brains barely had time to register what was happening before the troopers were in amongst them. Steel blades flashed, chopping at the lumbering forms. Slim Jim Bonita was cut down before a shot could be fired in defence.

Foggy Duke just managed to evade a slicing hay-maker that would have removed his head had the blow connected. Quickly drawing his pistol, he fired off three shots at the passing back of the blue-coated horse-man. One of them at least struck its target as the man yelled out, falling from the saddle. Duke grinned wolfishly.

'Got one of the bastards!' he yelled.

But another trooper immediately behind was not to be so denied. The point of his sabre skewered the little rodent's body right up to the hilt, forcing the attacker to release his grip. Duke staggered drunkenly, clutching the invasive object with both hands. A shot from the soldier's revolver finished the deadly task.

But Dutch Henry had not risen to his pre-eminent position in the ranks of Arizona's lawless breed without good reason.

Luckily for him, his bed-roll was positioned on the far side of fire in the shadow of some fallen tree trunks. Rolling out of sight, searching eyes quickly took in the dire situation. His first thought was for the woman. Her bed-roll was empty. A curse hissed from between gritted teeth. She had somehow been spirited away.

The gang leader called across for Jess Beaman to join him.

'Time we were out of here,' he muttered as the pair hunkered down behind the trunks. 'I don't know how they managed it, but these blue bellies have somehow tracked us down. And they've rescued the girl while we were sleeping.'

Beaman cursed. He couldn't care less about the dame. It was the loss of the gold that bothered him. He felt the urge to berate his leader for dragging the woman along. That could be debated over later. Their priority now was to slip away. The bulk of the gold would have to be abandoned.

A mirthless smirk cracked the outlaw's face. At least he'd had the foresight to salt enough away in his own pack to provide a grubstake should disaster strike.

But that all depended on them getting away.

The bulk of the fighting was taking place on the far side of the clearing. And it was obvious that the rest of the boys were not being given the chance to surrender. This was a revenge pursuit where death left its calling card. Some of them had tried to flee. But these soldier boys were taking no prisoners.

It was fortunate that the pincer movement had not included this side of the camp adjacent to the clump of palo verdes.

Without further ado, Dutch nudged his companion. Together they hugged the ground, crawling across to where the horses were picketed. Gently untying their own mounts, the two escapees led them into the cover of the trees. The dull light of the false dawn now became their saviour.

A glance behind informed Dutch that the soldiers were fully occupied in avenging their murdered comrades. Their surreptitious departure from the grizzly battlefield had not been witnessed.

Vandyke's only thought now was for escape.

Behind the knoll, Chad Gleeson was anxious to determine how the assault was progressing.

'Are you all right to be left down here while I check on the action?' he asked the schoolteacher, who was gradually recovering from the shock occasioned by her dire experience. A comb tugged at the dirt-caked hair straggling down her back. 'Squirrel-Tooth will keep you company.'

She nodded listlessly.

Leaving her with a gently reassuring squeeze of the shoulder down in the hollow, the lawman hustled back up the slope. He needed to see for himself if Dudley's attack was succeeding. The clash of steel intermingled with the rattle of small arms fire told of a deadly conflict. But who had gained the upper hand?

Scrambling up to the top of the rise, he held his breath. Nervous eyes peered over the lip. A sigh of relief whistled from tight lips when he saw that Ellis Dudley had taken the gang completely by surprise. Bodies were strewn about the camp as the soldiers went about their gruesome task of merciless retribution.

It was not a pretty sight. The observer was glad that Miss Calendar was not there to behold the macabre slaughter. It was the stuff of nightmares to which no innocent female should ever be subjected. Although not all had gone in the troopers' favour. A couple of bloodstained uniforms lay amidst the carnage.

A mopping-up operation was underway with the dismounted soldiers checking that none of the outlaws were left to tell the tale. A couple of groans were summarily despatched with sabres now dripping with blood.

The battle had lasted barely five minutes.

Gleeson was about to turn his back on the carnage when a slight movement in the corner of his eye commandeered his attention. From his elevated position on the knoll, he had a grandstand view of the battleground. Squinting into the gloom of the new day, he perceived two horses being led away on the far side of the tree cover. Those involved in the conflict could have no idea that two of the outlaws were escaping.

The sheriff clenched his teeth in fury as the two runaways mounted up and quickly spurred off along the floor of the canyon.

Seven-Up didn't need to assess the gambling odds. There could be only one response to this unexpected setback. Slithering back down the gravel slope, he hurried over to the woman.

'You will be in good hands here with Jones until Major Dudley returns,' he rasped out bluntly while saddling up his horse. 'I have to leave.'

'What has happened?' she asked in a nervous voice.

'Two of the critters have escaped,' he quickly informed her, tying off the cinch. 'I saw them from up yonder.' An arm brusquely indicated the rim of the knoll.

'Did you get a good look at them?' asked Jones.

'One was a big guy,' Gleeson replied. 'He wore a grey hat and had blond hair.'

'That was Dutch Henry,' the woman interjected, firmly adding, 'and was his associate a smaller man, stoutly built and with a red face and side whiskers?'

'Guess he was at that,' said the sheriff, impressed by this remarkable woman's acumen. 'You know who he was as well?'

'It has to be his second in command, Jess Beaman.'

So now he knew the identities of two absconders. And it just so happened that they were the two most dangerous members of the Vandyke gang. That made his task all the more hazardous. But there was no going back now. They had to be brought in to face justice, or face down over a saddle. Gleeson gave no thought to the notion that he might end up on the sharp end of a bullet.

'I'm going after them before they disappear into the maze of canyons to the south of here that make up the Mescal Mountains,' he announced, mounting up.

'Sure you don't need me with you, sheriff?' Jones enquired.

Gleeson shook his head. 'Best you stay here with Miss Calendar until the soldier boys return.'

'I'll tell the major where you have gone and what has happened,' the woman declared, adopting a soberly formal tone as befitted a schoolteacher. 'Do you want him to follow after you?'

'No!' he replied, impressed by her dignified manner. 'If'n I don't return within two days, he should head for

115

the nearest town and let the authorities know that Dutch Henry Vandyke is headed for the Mexican border. My reckoning is that he will first make for Coronado. That's a town about three days' ride west of here.'

Without further ado, he swung the horse around and made to spur off. Lucy Calendar stepped up to his horse and laid a restraining hand on his knee. Her touch sent a tingle through Gleeson's entire body. He shivered involuntarily as she peered up at him. The pair of big brown eyes swallowed him up in a poignant caress.

But the young woman herself remained totally unaware of the stimulating effect she was having on her tall, handsome liberator.

'You take care of yourself, Sheriff Gleeson,' she urged him. A deep concern was etched into the doleful gaze. 'I owe you a lot for putting your life on the line to rescue me from that braggart's clutches.'

The tough lawman, reduced to a quivering bowl of jelly, somehow managed to recover his equilibrium. 'Only doing my duty, ma'am,' he blurted out, struggling to suppress the hot flush suffusing his stubble-coated visage.

Not wanting to prolong the uncomfortable moment, he tipped a hand to his hat and swung away. It was some time before he was able to push Lucy Calendar's alluring features to the back of his mind. The capture of Dutch Henry and his sidekick would require all the guile and cunning he could muster.

ELEVEN

CONFRONTATION

Spurring his mount up through the dense stand of ponderosa pine cloaking the valley side, he eventually emerged above the treeline on to a plateau. From here he could follow the course which had been taken by Vandyke along the valley bottom.

Edging towards the rim of the mesa, he dismounted and scanned the terrain below. A broad, flat bottomland stretched away to the south. Twisting and turning like a giant serpent, the deep trench had numerous side canyons branching off at frequent intervals. The outlaws could take any one of these if they once suspected that a pursuer was on their tail.

Gleeson squinted out the glowing reflections cast by the rising sun. But the valley bottom was still cloaked in shadow. No movement could be detected with the human eye. In consequence he hauled out a telescope and placed it to his right eye. It was a vital piece of equipment retained from his army days. Focussing the magnifying lenses, he slowly swept the valley for any signs of movement.

Everything was still as the grave. Had the varmints hoodwinked him already?

He gripped the long tube in frustration. Again he swept the ground, this time much more slowly. That was when his straining eye caught the swishing tail of a horse disappearing behind a cluster of rocks. His whole body tensed. Estimating where the riders would emerge, he moved his telescope to the left. Two minutes later and the pair of riders sprang into view.

A long sigh issued from between tightly clenched teeth. They were sticking to the main trail to save time. Vandyke must have assumed that his escape had gone unnoticed. And so it would have had Gleeson not decided to check on the course of the battle being waged. Luck was on his side.

He could only trust that it would thus remain.

The destination of the two outlaws had to be the crossing of the Mescals by way of Jerusalem Pass. Gleeson shifted his gaze to bring up the notched cleft on the skyline. At their current pace, the two outlaws would reach the pass by the evening of the following day.

The lawman wanted to catch up before then. Once over Jerusalem Pass following an overnight rest, their speed would greatly increase on the downgrade, making it that much more difficult to overhaul them.

Packing away the scope, Gleeson remounted and set off. His elevated position provided the advantage of being able to trail the outlaws from a safe distance. The sun was high overhead when the duo finally stopped for a break. Once again, Gleeson took out his telescope to keep a close watch on the proceedings.

It soon became clear to the pursuer that this was no ordinary rest break. Judging by the men's body language, a fiery altercation was the cause. Unable to hear the gist of the verbal exchange, he could nonetheless see that a showdown was imminent. Prodding fingers and waving arms were not signs of a friendly conflab.

The sheriff's judicious assessment of the situation unfolding in the valley below had hit the nail on the head. Leaving the scene of the recent debacle behind, Jess Beaman was becoming increasingly riled.

He rapidly convinced himself that this calamity was all Vandyke's fault. It had all started when the gang boss insisted on robbing the stagecoach of gold bullion being transferred to the bank in Globe.

Going up against a military escort was a cockeyed plan. The Dutchman should have known that the army would not sit back and accept such a catastrophe without robust retaliation. And they had the means to carry out effective reprisals far beyond those of the regular law enforcement agencies.

The truth of that assertion had been proven in no uncertain terms. And it had been compounded by Vandyke's kidnapping of the schoolteacher. Beaman aimed a glowering snarl at the gang leader's back. He knew that the plan ought to have been challenged when it was first broached. But Dutch was a formidable leader and it would have taken a braver man than Jess

Beaman to go up against him.

Now his mind was made up. Once they were safe from pursuit, he intended parting company from his partner. The guy was bad whiskey.

A determined set to his craggy features indicated that a split was essential. And once he had cut loose, there was every chance of being able to form a new gang of his own someplace else, like Colorado or New Mexico. Then he would be the leader, and more than able to make a better job of it than this turkey.

The more Beaman thought about it, the more insistent became his need to confront the issue head on. He'd had a bellyful of knuckling under to Dutch Henry Vandyke.

The kidnapping of the woman had been the last straw.

'Haul up there, Dutch,' he called out in a brusque manner that immediately registered with the other man.

Vandyke had sensed that his partner was simmering, and not merely on account of their recent defeat. Beaman's contrary manner had been bothering him for some time. The guy always seemed to be questioning his decisions.

'Something on your mind, Jess?' he replied casually, hauling back on the reins.

'I'm cutting loose.' Beaman's announcement was candid and direct. 'You and me are finished. Going up against the army was madness. And you never did learn to separate business from pleasure. And this is where it's gotten us.'

'You talking about the dame?'

'Her and all the others you couldn't keep your hands off.'

The two men held each other's flinty gaze.

Vandyke considered the revelation before replying. His mouth turned down at the edges, implying his disappointment. The morose regard was matched by that of a jackrabbit peeping from behind a clump of saltbush.

'Rather a sudden decision, ain't it?' he proffered. 'Don't you think we ought to talk this over?'

'There's nothing to talk about,' Beaman shot back. 'You snarled things up good and proper by killing those troopers. I want no more part in your crazy schemes.'

Dutch's face turned a russet hue. But he kept his cool. A blank expression gave nothing away. The rabbit ducked out of sight, sensing bad vibes in the air.

'That so,' Vandyke nodded as if in acceptance of the declaration. He then skewered the other man with a bleak eye. 'You figure that Dutch Henry is gonna just roll over and let you run away?'

'Seems to me that you ain't got no choice in the matter,' Beaman retorted, making to swing his mount away.

'That's where you're wrong, buddy,' snarled Vandyke, nudging his own mount to block off Beaman's path. 'Nobody quits without my say-so. And I ain't given you the go-ahead.'

Beaman backed his horse up. He snarled out a lurid retort. At the same time a hand dropped to the holstered gun on his hip.

But Vandyke was ready. He had been expecting the move. A small Wesson twin-shot derringer appeared in his right hand. It had been fastened up the sleeve of his jacket. Unknown to anybody else in the gang, it had always been secreted there for just such an occasion as this. He had learned the lesson early on in his career from none other than Charley Swiftnick.

Both bullets spat from the small gun. At such close range they punched Beaman off the back of his horse. He didn't stand a chance. His body hit the ground. But the low-calibre shots had not killed him.

Staggering to his feet, he drew his own revolver.

Vandyke now palmed his revolver to finish the job. The sudden blast of gunfire panicked a flurry of cactus wrens, which rose into the air from their roost in a cluster of cholla.

The killer's blank features opened up into a broad grin of satisfaction.

Dismounting, he strode across to where Beaman's horse was idly chewing on some gramma grass as if nothing untoward had occurred.

'Thought I didn't know about the gold you'd stolen, eh, Jess?' he muttered to the still form of his ex-partner. 'I guess you figured it would give you a grubstake with me out of the way. Well, things sure didn't turn out how you'd planned. That lovely yellow peril is gonna buy me a new life now instead.'

He removed the saddle-bags and carried them across to his own horse.

'*Adios*, sucker,' he said, tipping his hat to the corpse. He then set off at the gallop, eager to make tracks.

Those shots could have been heard by the bluecoats.

The sudden and violent confrontation in the valley below had taken Chad Gleeson by surprise. But he quickly recovered from the shock.

This was a piece of good fortune upon which he intended to capitalize. Mounting up, he spurred off. His intention was to get down into the valley bottom and lay an ambush for the victorious winner of the conflict. Seven-Up's gambling intuition told him that the odds were now clearly in his favour.

A hundred yards further along the rim of the mesa, a narrow split worn down by eons of flash flooding offered a steep yet feasible way down to ground level.

Nudging his horse into the stony fissure, he made a chary descent. Fractured turrets of red sandstone rose up on either side of the dark ravine. Painstakingly assiduous, Gleeson held the sorrel on a tight rein. This was not a place for undue haste. One slip and disaster would be the inevitable result.

Heart in mouth, he descended the scree run, hoping that he would still be ahead of Vandyke on reaching the bottom. Finally on level ground, he quickly threw a probing glance up and down the trail. There was no sign of the outlaw. After checking the sandy floor for signs of any recent passage he was able to confirm that no human on horseback had ridden this way recently.

But the guy would be here soon enough. There was no time to lose in formulating a plan of action to arrest him. Many law officers would have been content to shoot first rather than take a man alive. They reckoned it saved them a wagonload of hassle. Tied over a saddle there was no chance of a corpse turning the tables on a tired lawman badly in need of sleep.

Seven-Up Gleeson was not one of those dudes. He had always given every felon apprehended an even break. It was the gambler in him. If'n the critter was foolish enough to resist, that altered things. Then he had no hesitation in using his guns to maximum effect.

At the point where he had come down into the valley, the trail passed through a clump of cottonwoods. That gave him an idea. Ensuring the sorrel was out of sight, he selected a tree where the main branch leaned out across the trail. His only problem with this scheme was that the approaching rider might well be travelling at a fast clip. Somehow he needed to be slowed down.

A smirk cracked Gleeson's face as he removed his broad-brimmed hat. Placing it on the trail a short distance beyond the tree, he then shimmied up the main trunk. A series of stretching and contorting of arms and legs found him concealed within the thick foliage. There he positioned himself on the branch, and settled down to await the arrival of his quarry.

Ten minutes passed before the solid rhythmic beat of an approaching horse cut through the gentle rustling of leaves. Gleeson hauled himself up on to his feet ready to greet the unsuspecting killer. Keeping out of sight he had little fear of being spotted. Only an alien sound would make the guy look up.

Gleeson held on to another branch to steady himself as the thud of hoofs drew nearer. Balancing himself ready for a drop on to the back of the rider, he tensed up, waiting for the guy to pass by underneath.

The approaching horse slowed its frantic pace. Vandyke had spotted the hat. The initial thought flitting through his brain was to question its sudden appearance in this remote wilderness.

He was given no further chance to speculate.

As soon as Vandyke had passed beneath the branch, Gleeson launched himself into the air. Landing on the horse's rump, his right arm snaked around the outlaw's neck. Both men tumbled off the horse on to the hard ground. Taken completely unawares, Vandyke was slow to react. His assailant wasted no time in frivolous challenges for his quarry to surrender peaceably. Whipping out his pistol he clubbed the guy over the head, effectively neutralizing any resistance.

Dutch Henry slumped to the ground, out cold. Gleeson soon had him handcuffed and tied to a tree. It was already late in the afternoon so he decided this was as good a place as any to make camp for the night.

Soon a fire was burning upon which sat the coffee pot bubbling merrily. The brew had fully percolated before the prisoner regained consciousness. A series of groans heralded the outlaw's return to the realization that he was no longer a free agent.

A watery eye opened. Sitting opposite was his abductor. Vandyke's mouth twisted on seeing that he had been outfoxed by that darned tinstar.

But Dutch Henry was not one to accept his unwelcome situation lightly. 'That there coffee smells mighty inviting, sheriff,' he remarked with a wan smile. 'Any chance of a cup?' He held his hands up, hoping the lawman would release the cuffs.

'Sure, Dutch,' replied Gleeson with an equal measure of aplomb. 'But I'll be feeding you, just like a baby.'

The outlaw's nonchalant demeanour slipped. He growled out a threat.

'Think you can hold on to Dutch Henry Vandyke, Mr?' He grunted with disdain. 'Ain't a lawman alive that can do that.'

'So tell me, Dutch,' replied Gleeson, sipping his coffee and puffing on a cigar. 'Just how exactly are you gonna escape? I'd be interested to hear, seeing as I have no intention of releasing you, for any reason. You want to take a leak? Do it in your pants. You're going on trial for murder and kidnapping, not to mention highway robbery. There again, once we get back to the place where the army are camped, I can always hand you over to them.'

That threat was enough to scare the Dutchman into silence. The blood drained from his face at the thought of what those bluecoats would do if'n this sheriff decided that a trial was too much trouble. He felt his innards churning up with fear.

Thoroughly abashed, his spirit cowed, the outlaw muttered, 'All right, you win. I won't cause you any trouble. Just make sure I get back to civilization in one piece.'

TWELVE

BREAK-OUT

It was now almost three years to the day since the outlaw had been convicted of his crimes and sentenced to a twenty stretch in the notorious Arizona prison at Yuma. The judge had enjoyed sending the killer down with the stipulation that the sentence should include hard labour.

The Dutchman had not taken the judgment with his usual display of nonchalant disdain. Threats had been flung out, all aimed at the nemesis who had brought him in.

'I'll get out of there someday,' he had railed as the guards dragged him out of the courtroom. 'And when I do, you'd better watch your back, mister.'

That warning had stuck with the killer throughout his incarceration at Yuma. It was the one notion that had kept him going. The resolution that one day he would get out and avenge himself on the skunk he blamed for ruining his life. Yet only recently had Vandyke figured out a way of escaping from the infamous prison.

Although others had spoken out at his trial, it was Sheriff Chad Gleeson's evidence that had swung the jury against him. The guy had enjoyed watching the defendant squirm in the dock as he replayed the course of events. And to add insult to injury, he had since learned that Gleeson had married the schoolteacher. That news really sealed the lawman's fate in Vandyke's twisted mind.

'So how are you planning to get us out of this hell-hole?'

The question came from a granite-faced tough. Davy Dewer, known as the Hunter, claimed to hold the record for shooting the most bears in a month back in his native Tennessee. The cane-breaker had come west to seek his fortune when the game ran out. Hunter swung his hammer at yet another rock, which disintegrated with a mighty crack. His remark was aimed at Dutch Henry.

The convict stared into the distance. His bleak gaze was focussed on some obscure point on the far side of the quarry where the others were labouring in a huge hole in the ground located some three miles from the prison. Generations of convicts had laboured under the hot sun to hack out rocks that were then crushed into gravel used in the construction industry.

Another con who was among Dutch's inner circle prodded their natural-born leader for information. Since Dutch had intimated the aspiration to his three buddies, their interest had been peaked. Even though the prison authorities claimed it was escape-proof, Dutch was convinced that any place could be breached if'n you had the urge.

And he now reckoned to have found the chink in Yuma's armour. Any chance of shucking the fetters of the ghastly hole was like nectar to the gods.

'Am I gonna get to top that bastard, Andrews, for what he done to me?' snarled Snow Labone.

Barely out of his teens, the young tough looked twenty years older because of his shock of white hair. He had saved Dutch's life when a fellow con had tried to knife him, claiming he had stolen some tobacco. But the slugging of the bruiser had earned Snow ten lashes on the Wheel administered by the sadistic warder.

The nudge on the Dutchman's arm brought him out of his reverie.

'All in good time, boys,' he said with a cheeky grin while hefting his own hammer. 'I'll tell you all the details when we're on recreation tonight.'

'No talking over there!' rapped one of the guards, wielding his billy club with menacing intent. 'Any more warnings and I'll stick you all in the Sweat Box.'

The notorious punishment cell was nought but a hole in the ground. But it received the full force of the blistering Arizona sun. Two or three days of that and you were lucky to emerge alive.

The fourth member of the group growled out a rabid retort.

'What was that, Tachoma?' snapped the guard, lifting his club aggressively. 'You answering back? Maybe a session on the Wheel will teach you some respect for your betters.'

Whispers Tachoma squared his broad back. He was head and shoulders taller than the puny custodian. A flick of his muscle-bound arms could have broken the guy's back. But Dutch Henry quickly stepped in to calm the storm-tossed waters. Luckily, the croaking grunt that passed for Tacoma's vocal delivery muted his outburst. He had lost the full use of his voice in a knife fight. The slash had severed his voice box.

'My buddy only asked if'n he could have a drink of water, boss.' Dutch wiped a hand across his sweating brow. 'Sure is hotter than the devil's kitchen out here.'

The intervention did the trick, diverting attention on to something else.

'You lazy faggots will take a drink at rest break and not before, got that?'

'Sure thing, boss,' opined an obsequious Dutch Henry, pushing Tachoma away. 'Anything you say, boss.' Then to his cronies with a wry wink, he added, 'You heard Mr Henshaw, boys. Now let's get back to work and earn our supper.'

Evincing a supercilious smirk, the guard sniffed before ambling away to accost some other poor saps.

'Now there's one bastard that I could cheerfully strangle with his own necktie and enjoy every second of it,' rasped Tachoma, aiming a globule of sandy spit at the guard's retreating back.

'You need to be more patient, Whispers,' chided Vandyke casually. 'Everything comes to him who waits.'

'Well, I've waited long enough already,' replied the

irate convict. 'You sure you have a plan, Dutch?'

Vandyke responded with a crafty grin while tapping his nose. The heavy lump hammer swung before crashing down to earth. The ground shook as fragments of broken rock and dust joined the rest of the day's gravel target.

The others joined in, rivulets of sweat glistening on their bronzed torsos. If nothing else, the back-breaking toil had removed all excess flesh and made them fit. Ready for anything Dutch Henry had in mind.

Another week passed before circumstances were ripe for the proposed jailbreak.

Once a week, a locomotive hauling freight wagons arrived at the quarry to be loaded with crushed gravel. Only a selected few convicts were assigned to the gruelling task. It was not a popular job. So Dutch Henry did not want to appear over-eager in volunteering for a task that nobody else wanted.

All his persuasive acumen was required to wheedle him and his buddies on to the labour gang. The ploy involved announcing to other cons that he and his buddies had no intention of working on that miserable gang. At the time they were in what passed for the recreation room. In truth it was a large cell with some tables and chairs where cons could play cards for an hour each evening before lockdown.

'No way would we do it, not even for double rations. That right boys?' he scoffed out loud to his associates.

'Too darned right, Dutch,' the Hunter agreed, squaring his shoulders. He handed a stringy rabbit leg to his sidekick. 'That job is for screwballs only.'

131

Dutch chewed on the gristly meat. It never ceased to amaze him how Dewer managed to snare the creatures out here in the desert. But that was why they called him the Hunter. And at least these regular offerings helped to supplement the monotonous diet of mealy grits.

The conversation had been deliberately conducted within the hearing of Warden Andrews, knowing what his reaction would be.

'Well, now,' drawled the bestial guard. A mirthless smirk revealed teeth blackened by baccy-chewing. Andrews meaningfully tapped the heavy club in the palm of his hand. 'You guys ain't gonna do no loading this week, that so?'

The four convicts spun round. Fearful shock at having been overheard was painted across their faces.

'We didn't mean nothing, Mr Andrews, honest,' whined Vandyke. 'Just thinking aloud, is all.'

'Too bad, suckers,' snarled the guard. 'Your names will be put at the head of this week's list.' He tapped his chest with the club. 'It's me that decides who does what in this place. You miserable cons have no rights unless I say so. Got that?'

The four men looked down at the floor, suitably abashed. With his beaky snout sniffing the air, Andrews strutted off. A pleased expression warped his hard features. Once he was out of earshot, derisive sniggers pursued the gullible custodian.

'Easy as falling off a log,' crowed Whispers Tachoma.

'Some guys just ain't gotten the brains,' concurred Labone, shaking his mat of greasy white hair with glee.

'It sure was our lucky day teaming up with you, Dutch,'

observed the Hunter in a respectful tone of voice.

The others nodded their avid accord with that heart-felt sentiment.

Vandyke preened under the gushing array of com-pliments. 'You guys stick with me once we get out of this dump,' he proposed, 'and I'll make you all rich.'

The success of his plan depended on bribing four other convicts to join the loading gang towards the end of the shift. Their job would be to take the places of the absconders, thus ensuring that guards made the final count tally.

Tobacco was the key to obtaining their co-operation. It was the principal source of wealth in any prison. Some weeks before, Dutch had ensured that his boys stopped smoking and conserved their supplies. Questions had been deftly parried. His only concession to their curiosity had been a pledge that it was all part of his escape plans.

The days prior to the proposed breakout dragged interminably. Dutch had to remind his men to act nor-mally so as not to arouse any suspicions among the guards, or indeed the other convicts. Secrecy was a prime element of any successful caper.

Their nerves were strung tighter than a maiden's corset when the day finally came around. All their com-bined efforts were needed to remain outwardly calm.

The loading was no less onerous than they had expected. A brutally laborious chore, but one they rel-ished. Knuckling down with a firm resolve, the prospect that this would be their last day of captivity helped lighten the burden. The plan relied on the fact that no count was made of those convicts labouring in the quarry. This was because there was no place for them to go except into the desert. Any absconders would easily be caught, or die of thirst in the unforgiving heat of the Imperial Desert.

The arrival of the freight train was a different matter entirely, hence the need for an official count of those involved in the gravel shipment.

It was easy for the others involved in the escape to mingle with the loading gang during one of the few rest breaks. The extra men would not be noticed while they were working. They could later disperse into the prison before the escape was discovered.

Finally, the whistle blew, signalling the end of the gruelling shift.

Dutch and his crew were at the far end of the line. A couple of their co-conspirators started an argument which distracted the attention of the guards. With their backs turned, Dutch and the others quickly clambered aboard the wagons and buried themselves under the mounds of gravel.

Shouts and threats from the guards quickly broke up the fracas, enabling the count to proceed. Moments later with all the men accounted for, the line of convicts moved off back into the quarry. Dutch peeped out through the slats of the wagon. It had worked. His plan had succeeded. He felt like cheering aloud, but contained his exultation to a bunched fist pummelling the palm of his hand.

A wailing hoot penetrated the dusty fog enveloping the escapers. That was the engineer announcing the imminent departure of the freight train. Lurching forward, the line of wagons shuffled off on its journey north.

Dutch held his breath. He desperately issued prayers to a God he had long since abandoned that no last-minute hitch would herald the discovery of the escape. The train gradually picked up speed with no panic-stricken shouts of alarm. After ten minutes he felt able to breathe again normally.

Dutch Henry Vandyke had successfully accomplished what nobody had ever previously managed. Now he could concentrate on getting his revenge.

THIRTEEN

A DOWNER FOR SEVEN-UP

The delicious aroma of freshly ground coffee permeated the store. Chad Gleeson, wearing a clean overall as befitted the prosperous owner of a dry goods emporium, operated the handle of the grinder. He was serving a rather stout lady of middle years who was busy checking her purchases.

'How is Linus today, Mrs Wikeley?' he asked, filling a bag with the coffee. 'I hope he has been taking the doctor's advice.'

'The old goat would be out of bed and hopping around if I didn't watch him,' grumbled the woman. 'He hates being laid up with that broken leg.'

'You tell him from me to do as he's told,' counselled Chad, a serious expression on his clean-shaven face. 'For a guy his age, it'll take another month before he's fit to walk unaided.'

'I sure will, Chad. He'll listen if I tell him you said he should take it easy.' Emma Wikeley paid for her goods and was turning to leave when she asked, 'And how is Lucy faring with that new baby? It's due soon, ain't it?'

'Another two weeks.'

'Then you tell her from me that she should take it easy as well.'

Chad nodded as they both burst out laughing.

As the door of the emporium closed on his latest customer, Chad was given a few moments to reflect on his good fortune. He had been running the store for near enough two and a half years.

After the trial of Dutch Henry Vandyke, Chad had wasted no time in courting the new schoolteacher. Their relationship blossomed over the forthcoming months. But Lucy Calendar refused to place it on a more permanent footing while her beau was still working as the county sheriff. She thought it was too dangerous an occupation for a married man.

The lawman was in a quandary. He loved the job, but knew that unless he gave it up he would lose her. And that was not an option he relished.

As a result he resigned. There was enough money stashed away for him to buy a dry goods store that had recently come on the market. It was a going concern and the owner taught him all the rudiments before the business changed hands.

He had not regretted the decision. Marriage to Lucy had inevitably followed. And for the first time in his life, he felt safe and secure. Gone were the days of looking over his shoulder wondering if some brigand was waiting to gun him down, never knowing whether that day would be your last. It was an exciting life, no doubt about that, but highly nerve-wracking and insecure.

There were odd times at the beginning when he hankered after the old days, the exhilaration of pursuing villains and bringing them in. But those occasions were now few and far between. He was as contented as any man had a right to be.

And with a child on the way, a guard angel was indeed smiling down on him.

Vandyke was locked up in Yuma Penitentiary. The critter was lucky not to have been sentenced to hang. Clearly the presiding judge on that day must have been feeling benevolent. Twenty years' hard labour was a long time. Likely he would end his days there.

Chad was unpacking some bolts of cloth that had just been delivered when a boy entered the store. The kid slapped the newspaper on the counter. Feeling generous, Chad rewarded him with a stick of candy.

'Gee thanks, Mr Gleeson.' The boy smiled, eagerly sucking on the sugary treat. He jabbed a finger at the paper's bold headline. 'Some bad guys have escaped from Yuma. First time I ever heard of that happening.'

He didn't wait for any comment from the store-keeper as he bustled outside to deliver the rest of that week's edition of the *Arizona Herald*.

Chad didn't pay the remark much heed. But then curiosity, blended with a touch of concern, found his eyes scanning the headline. It read: *Notorious Outlaw Escapes From Yuma*. No name was mentioned. So Chad read the article. What he discovered sent a chill down his spine. Three years into his sentence and Dutch Henry Vandyke was free. And he had taken three other convicts with him.

Suddenly the nerve-jangling threat of retribution against Sheriff Chad Gleeson leapt into stark focus. At the time, the threat had been disregarded as the raving of a sore loser. Now it appeared all too real.

Automatically, Chad's hand strayed down to the drawer below the counter. He pulled it open and removed the gun belt and holstered Colt Frontier. Flexing his hand, he withdrew the gun from its oiled holster. The heavy weight seemed unfamiliar. This was the first time he had handled any firearm since quitting as sheriff over two years before.

His wife had insisted that no firearms be allowed on the premises. Not even her traumatic experience in the company of the Vandyke gang had altered that view. Indeed it had strengthened her resolve that all those who toted guns were reckless individuals.

She had no idea that her husband had retained his revolver. A quick glance behind to their living quarters assured him that Lucy was still visiting with the midwife who was shortly expected to deliver their infant.

Strapping on the gun belt, he tried cocking and drawing the weapon. It was obvious from the start that a lot of practice would be required to bring him up to his old level of dexterity. And time was not on his side.

The newspaper report stated that Vandyke had absconded, ostensibly on a freight train, over a month before. So why had it taken so long for the news to

139

come out? The rest of the article provided the answer.
It had transpired that the prison governor had tried to
conceal the escape to save face. But the men he had
sent to hunt down the fugitives had failed to locate
them.

The governor was then forced to admit defeat. He
had since been replaced and the whole system of hard
labour overhauled.

With that thought in his mind, Gleeson knew that his
nemesis could be arriving in Casa Grande anytime
soon. Again he reached down to the drawer under the
counter, this time extracting a bottle of whiskey. A liberal
slug of the hard liquor stabbed at the back of his throat.

So, he surmised. What course of action should be
taken?

Since Chad had resigned as the permanent law
officer in the town, the council had made do with a
system of part-time incumbents for the post. In the
beginning, they had appointed a gunslinger who had
advertised himself as a private detective. The skunk had
defrauded the town by absconding with all the rents
collected during his first month in office.

That was when they decided that each of them
should hold the office for a limited period to save
money. Casa Grande was a peaceable town in which
nothing much happened to validate the need for a
town marshal. Chad had been a county sheriff, which
meant his responsibilities were more far-reaching.

Removing his overalls, he closed up the store and
hurried across to the temporary marshal's office.

'You seem in an all-fired hurry, Chad,' declared the

current member of the council to sport a tin star. It was Jacob Randle, who still operated the town's meat emporium. 'What's bothering you?'

There was no hiding the nervous look on the ex-lawman's face. He threw down the newspaper. 'Read this,' he said, jabbing a finger at the front-page article.

The butcher quickly scanned the gist of the report before shrugging his shoulders. 'What has this got you so fired up about?'

A sour twist parted Gleeson's lips as he rapped out, 'You may not recall, marshal.' The inflection contained a thick dose of sarcasm. 'But the varmint threatened that one day he would return and get even with me for putting him away.'

Randle stroked his chin. 'Seems I do recollect some such words being exchanged. But it was all hot air. He wouldn't dare come back now.'

'You reckon?' huffed Gleeson. 'Maybe that's because it ain't your life that's on the line. I know Vandyke. And he's gonna want his pound of flesh. And it's my skin that he's after ventilating with a six-shooter.'

This was Randle's first major incident while holding down the unwanted office of temporary lawman. And if a situation was likely to develop involving gunplay as Gleeson had suggested, then he wanted no part of it.

After prevaricating somewhat, he then offered the suggestion that Gleeson should leave town until the danger blew over. 'If the skunk does come looking for you, he'll soon depart when he finds you ain't living here no more.'

'And what about my wife?' protested Gleeson, waving

141

his arms in frustration. 'She's due to give birth soon. I can't leave her now.'

'Then take her with you.'

'Some marshal you are,' snapped Gleeson. 'I want protection and help. And all you want is to get rid of the problem. I should have known from before what sort of lily-livered towrag you were.'

Randle lurched to his feet. 'There's no need for insults. I've made my suggestion,' he replied pompously. 'And you can be sure that it will be backed up by the rest of the council when I tell them. We don't want any trouble in Casa Grande. This is your problem, not ours.'

Gleeson stamped out of the office, slamming the door loudly in his aggravation. This town hadn't changed at all. Everything was fine and dandy until trouble came a-calling. Then nobody wanted to know. It was the same when he had tried to raise that posse to track down the Vandyke gang. Gleeson cursed his foolishness for thinking these people would help him in his hour of need.

Muttering to himself, he stumbled across the street back to his store. So intent was Gleeson's mind fixed on berating that cowardly excuse for a marshal that the irate ex-sheriff was almost run down by a horseman.

'Whoa there, Seven-Up!' chided the rider, dragging his horse away from the preoccupied pedestrian. The animal whinnied, stamping his hoofs and frothing at the mouth at the sudden jolt. 'You'll get yourself killed crossing the street like that.'

Gleeson looked up. 'Gonna happen anyways if'n I

can't get my gun hand back into shape,' he mumbled, flexing the aberrant item.

'What in thunder are you talking about?' Squirrel-Tooth Jones quizzed. He was puzzled by his old buddy's strange conduct. It was completely out of character. 'I thought you'd given up all that legal stuff when you married Lucy.'

For his part in the capture of Dutch Henry Vandyke, Frank Jones had been suitably rewarded. And not only with a share of the cash bounty on the killer's head. His boss, Harvey Proctor, had been so impressed with the cowpoke's actions that he had promoted the kid to the leading hand with the Rising Sun outfit. Frank and the ex-sheriff often met up for some hands of their favourite game in the saloon.

Gleeson shook his head. 'He's coming back.'

'Who is?' Jones questioned rather testily. 'You ain't making no sense, man.'

'Vandyke has escaped from Yuma,' Gleeson blurted out, effectively stunning the cowboy, whose jaw dropped open with shock. 'And I'm certain that he's on his way here to kill me. Remember what he said at the trial?'

'I sure do,' agreed Jones, recovering his voice. 'But like you, I figured he was all mouth, seeing as he was down for a twenty-year stretch.'

'None of these spineless critters running the town will help,' grumbled Gleeson. 'They want me to leave town. If'n I did that, it would mean going on the run until he caught up with me. And with Lucy expecting, ain't no way I'm doing that.'

'So you are intending to face him?'

'I ain't been given no choice.' Gleeson's shoulders slumped in dejection at his unwelcome predicament. 'On my own if'n I have to.'

Not wishing to prolong the uncomfortable discussion any further, he continued on his way back to the store.

Jones watched until the bowed form disappeared into the store. The chastened cowpoke nudged his mount down the street towards the butcher's shop. He had been sent into town to investigate the rumour that Jacob Randle was stocking his butcher's shop with meat from rustled cattle. Some hides had been discovered at the local tannery sporting the Rising Sun's distinctive brand.

But first he needed a drink to mull over the disturbing news from his old comrade.

Pushing through the doors of the Tomahawk Saloon, he idly sauntered up to the bar. His face displayed a dour and crestfallen guise. It was a distinctly unusual trait for the typically amiable cowhand. The bartender immediately picked up on his new customer's glum mood.

'What's bugging you, Squirrel-Tooth?' he breezed, pulling the guy his normal jar of beer. 'Look like you've lost a silver dollar and found a wooden nickel.'

'Just heard some bad news,' Jones muttered, sinking half the pot in a single draught.

'And what might that be?' pressed the 'keep, polishing some glasses.

'A few years back before you arrived in Casa Grande, there was a big trial here,' Jones explained. 'A killer by the name of Dutch Henry Vandyke was sentenced to twenty years in Yuma for numerous crimes.'

'Yeah, I heard about that while I was working the Black Dog up in Flagstaff,' interjected the ruddy-faced barman, waiting for the cowboy to continue.

'Well, the critter has escaped.' The barman shrugged. Yuma was a long way from Casa Grande. 'And at his trial he threatened to kill the guy that put him inside.' Still the barman showed little interest.

'So what has that to do with you?' he asked when Jones sunk back into his morose disposition.

'I was in the posse that captured him along with Chad Gleeson.'

'You mean. . . ?' The barman was now all ears.

'That's right, he's coming here to settle some unfinished business.'

Three men leaning against the far end of the bar had been avidly listening to the discourse. One of them now pushed himself erect and turned to face the cowboy. The guy was a man mountain. A black beard of unkempt hair added to the aura of menace. His intimidating presence was further enhanced by the macabre growl of a voice sounding like a rusty door hinge.

'And he ain't alone,' the big man rapped out. The other two now joined the bulky form of Whispers Tachoma. Together they faced Jones in a line, hands poised above tied-down holsters.

Jones stepped back a pace, his face ashen.

A white-haired youngster jabbed a finger at the cowboy. 'You tell this fella that Dutch will be arriving on the noon stage,' Snow Labone sneered. 'If'n he's got any backbone he'll be there to face his judgment day.'

'Dutch aims to take this guy in a fair fight,' added Davy Dewer, hefting his long gun. 'We are just here to make certain no one else interferes.'

'You got that, buddy?' rasped Tachoma.

Jones merely nodded. But he couldn't move. His boots felt as if they were filled with lead.

'Then you best push along and give him the good news,' commented Tachoma with a dry laugh that rumbled like a leaking steam pump inside his lacerated throat. At the same time he palmed his revolver and sent a couple of slugs into the floorboards, missing the cowboy's boots by a whisker.

That was enough to animate Jones as the others joined in the fun. Hoots of laughter pursued the hapless cowpoke as he rapidly exited the saloon. His trip to the tannery and a confrontation with the temporary marshal was forgotten as he hustled along the boardwalk to Gleeson's emporium.

Bursting through the door, he was confronted by Randle and Mayor Stoker. Both of the officials were vehemently urging the storekeeper to accept their financial incentive to leave town immediately.

'This will get you started up someplace else,' pressed Stoker, pushing a wad of notes at Lucy Gleeson. 'I am sure you know it makes sense, Mrs Gleeson. It's not that we're afraid to help you, Chad.'

'We are just thinking about you and the new baby,' interposed Randle.

'After all, we're just businessmen, not gun hands.'

Jones had heard enough.

'Don't listen to these yellow rats, Chad,' he snapped. 'They are just trying to save their own miserable hides. I'll stand by you.'

Gleeson had been momentarily swayed, tempted by the generous offer. His buddy's intervention now stiffened his resolve to stand firm.

'You heard the man,' Gleeson snarled. 'Take your blood money and stuff it where the sun don't shine.'

Snorting with indignation, the two councillors left the store.

Jones waited until they had departed before addressing his buddy. He then quickly relayed what had transpired in the saloon.

Lucy was not so reckless in her deliberations. She urged her husband to accept the council's bribe. 'It's a good offer and you haven't used a gun in years. You won't stand a chance going up against a hardened gunslinger like Vandyke. And I don't trust him at all.' She spat out her indignation. 'Fair fight? A guy like that doesn't know the meaning of the word.'

Chad slowly picked up the gun belt that was lying on a chair and buckled it around his waist. 'If'n I were to run now, Lucy,' he muttered solemnly, 'I'd never forgive myself. Seven-Up is my nickname. I've always taken a gamble on life's chequered course. And this one is the biggest of the lot.'

'Just remember that there'll be two of us out there,' Jones asserted, issuing the blunt reminder. His prominent molars clicked nervously as he fingered his six-gun. 'We're partners again, ain't we?'

'That was a long time ago, Squirrel-Tooth,' Gleeson

cautioned. 'You certain about this? Those guys are gonna come out shooting. And it won't matter who gets in their way just so long as I end up chewing dirt.'

'I was in this at the start,' Jones snapped back. 'And I'll be in at the finish.'

'Is there nothing I can say that will change your mind?' Lucy knew that she was fighting a losing battle when Chad responded with a doleful look of apology.

Stifling a pained grimace of reluctance, she gripped her husband's hand and squeezed it. Then she turned and made her way back upstairs. Tears welled in her eyes, dribbling down her cheeks. Chad could be stubborn and ornery when the mood took him. And if truth be told, she was scared stiff for him.

But deep down she was also proud to be his wife.

At the top of the stairs she swung round. 'Good luck to you both,' she said. 'And give that skunk a lead sandwich from me.' Then she was gone.

Chad looked at the clock ticking away on the wall. It read 11.45. Fifteen minutes to go. Each second resonated inside his head like a time bomb waiting to explode. He sucked in a lungful of air, hitched up his gun belt and headed for the door.

FOURTEEN

DAY OF THE RECKLESS GUN

Checking their guns, the two men went out into the noonday sun.

Everything looked bright and alive, except for the fact that there was nobody else in sight. News of the forthcoming showdown had spread rapidly. Gleeson and his buddy stood in the middle of the empty thoroughfare facing towards where the stagecoach was due to arrive in – another glance at his watch read 11.57 – three minutes' time.

Doubtless there were many eyes peeping out from behind blinds and shutters, all eager to watch the fray but equally keen to avoid getting involved. The two men squared their shoulders. Legs apart, their hands flexed ready to meet the menacing challenge laid down by the Dutch outlaw and his new gang.

Midday arrived along with the weekly stagecoach. Spot on time as usual. Two passengers alighted, neither of which was Dutch Henry Vandyke. Gleeson frowned. Surely all his concerns had not been self-initiated, all in his head. Jones had been warned in the saloon to expect nothing less than a clash of arms.

The stagecoach, having delivered its passengers and some cargo, then departed in a cloud of dust. Next stop Mesa to the north.

Total quietness descended over the waiting township. Not a sound disturbed the outwardly tranquil ambience. Even the birds had deserted the battleground. Gleeson threw a quizzical look at his partner. 'You sure those guys in the Tomahawk weren't just having fun at your expense?' He waved an arm, indicating the empty street.

'That was no joke, Chad,' Jones emphasized bluntly. 'They were deadly serious.'

Further speculation on this strange turn of events was busted apart by a flurry of pounding hoof beats from the opposite end of town. The ground shook as the two men spun on their heels. Four riders galloping in line abreast thundered down the street. The exposed duo were given no time to think as four guns opened fire on them. Bullets slammed into the dirt inches from their feet.

Instinctively, Gleeson pushed his buddy to the right while he dived left, scrambling for cover behind a handy water trough. The riders pounded by, yelling out shrieks of manic delight.

'Yahooooo!'

Dutch Henry had always displayed a reckless streak. It had paid off most of the time. And he now figured a direct frontal assault was the best way of achieving his warped ambition. The gang boss cackled insanely as his horse thundered by.

'Prepare to meet your maker, sheriff,' he hollered. 'Death in the form of Dutch Henry Vandyke has come to claim his dues.'

Gleeson managed to snap off a couple of shots at the disappearing backs. But the assailants were half hidden by the rising dust shroud and the bullets went wide.

Now his blood was up, coursing through tight veins like a mountain torrent. He felt an old exhilaration bursting forth. This was just like old times. Long-abandoned skills of pursuing lawless felons suddenly flowed back into his tingling frame. His gun hand flexed, at one with the familiar feel of the revolver.

The hunt was on.

He signalled to Jones to make his way up that side of the street taking full advantage of the cover offered by the buildings. Gleeson ran up the stairs of the Prairie Dog Hotel to the first-floor veranda. Holding the high ground was a military manoeuvre that gave instant advantage. Body bent low, he ran to the far end.

A figure was emerging from an alley on the far side towards which Jones was slowly edging. Another few steps and the killer would catch him unawares. Taking careful aim with his Frontier Colt .44, the ex-lawman lined up the unsuspecting bruiser in his sights.

Somewhere in the mad dash along the street, Snow Labone had lost his hat. His white hair now offered a clear target.

Gleeson's pistol exploded. Two shots rang out just as the young tough figured he had the cowboy at his mercy. One clipped the wooden veranda post near his head, but the second punched him against the wall of the undertaker's.

A fitting place to end his days.

Jones halted as the bushwacker pitched forward into the street.

But Gleeson was not the only one in Casa Grande to have seen military action. A rifle barked from the roof of a building across the street. The bullet from a Winchester carbine would have finished the contest for Gleeson had he not been wearing his Sunday hat.

The metal conchos affixed to the hatband deflected the lethal slug enough to thwart the grim reaper's depredations. Nonetheless, it scored a furrow along the side of his head. Thankfully it was only a surface wound but it still felt like a red-hot poker seering his scalp. The shock jerked the ex-lawman back.

He tumbled into the room through an open window just in time to spot the terrified incumbent cowering behind a chest of drawers. Gleeson stumbled to his feet, blood dribbling down his face from the laceration.

Removing his bandanna, he tied it round his head.

'Sorry to intrude,' came the casual response. 'Somebody out there doesn't seem to like me.' Then he peered around the edge of the frame to get a bead on the roof shooter.

Jones had seen the attack on his friend. With reckless disregard for his own safety, he dashed into the street and let fly with his pistol until it clicked on empty. The sudden retaliation was enough to drive the varmint down under cover. That gave Gleeson the opportunity to exit the room and hustle back to the end of the veranda and down the stairs to ground level.

A movement at the corner of an alley two blocks north caught his attention. Shots were exchanged between the participants but none found their mark. Slivers of wood were chewed from a wooden signboard above Gleeson's head.

'You can't escape your destiny, Gleeson.' Vandyke's chilling declaration echoed down the street. It sent a shiver down the ex-lawman's spine. Shrugging off the nauseous feeling, he called across to his sidekick.

'Head down to the Hooray Corral. We'll make our final stand there.' A nod of acknowledgement from Jones and he backed down the street, reloading his gun while keeping a watchful eye for any signs of the pro-tagonists.

The corral was on the edge of Casa Grande. A fenced enclosure with a barn at one end. The two men made it without mishap, ducking inside the gloomy interior.

'That guy on the roof nearly took you out, Chad,' observed Jones, pointing at the bloodstained bandana.

'My Sunday hat didn't come out so good though,' grumbled Gleeson, poking a finger through the torn fabric.

Jones smiled. 'I'll buy you a new one when we're done with these varmints.'

The two men exchanged nervous smiles. They were positioned on either side of the double doors which faced the main street down which their adversaries were gingerly progressing. 'Keep them busy while I go up into the loft. I'll have a better chance to pick them off from up there.'

A desultory exchange of fire began. The random trading of lead continued for a further ten minutes. Gleeson was content to keep the assailants pinned down indefinitely. He knew that a wild character like Dutch Henry would quickly become frustrated by the status quo.

And so it proved. A muttered series of orders saw two of the attackers zig-zagging across the street. They were taking advantage of any available cover to get closer to the corral.

One of them was a big guy with a heavy black beard. But in a gunfight like this, the bulky size of Whispers Tachoma was a marked hindrance. It slowed him down. He made a sudden dash to the corner of the corral. Halfway across the open ground a bullet from Jones's rifle caught him in the throat. The bullet stopped him in his tracks.

Jones let out a yell of triumph. His partner kept an eye on the buckskin-clad Davy Dewer, who was far more agile and a clearly experienced hunter. The guy disappeared from view, leaving the gang boss alone. But Vandyke was hidden behind the last building on the edge of town. And he was out of range for a handgun.

Just then, a scream of pain cut through the fetid atmosphere of the barn. It had come from below. Squirrel-Tooth must be in trouble. Scrambling across the straw-filled upper floor, he peered down through the trapdoor. Bulging eyes revealed his buddy pinned to the barn door by a twin-pronged pitchfork.

The Hunter was on the other end of the lethal implement. He had managed to sneak round the back of the barn where an open window had enabled him to silently creep up on the unsuspecting cowpoke. Grasping hold of a pitchfork he must have crept up on Jones and surprised him. It was only because Dewer accidentally nudged a loose harness that his presence was revealed.

Jones turned and just had time to avoid the fatal thrust of the sharp prongs. All the same, his arm was skewered to the door.

Dewer frantically tugged at the pitchfork, trying to jerk it free for the final lunge. That gave Gleeson sufficient time to make his challenge.

'Drop that fork and step back,' The blunt command momentarily stayed the Hunter's frenzied efforts to finish the job he had started. He looked up to see a six-gun pointing at his belly.

When he escaped from Yuma, Davy Dewer promised himself that he would never return. Surrendering now would mean a one way trip to Hell. His hand reached for the holstered revolver slung round his waist.

'Don't do it!'

But the brusque retort was ignored. The escaped convict was past the point of no return. His gun rose and swivelled round to deliver its load. But it was Gleeson's gun that roared. Davy Dewer had made his final hunting trip. At least he would not be returning to Yuma.

The man from Tennessee was ignored as Gleeson sought to extricate his young associate from his pointed dilemma. There was no easy way to release him.

'Bite on this,' Gleeson advised, handing over a stray piece of leather. 'I'll have to yank it out quick.'

Girding himself to the task, Gleeson sucked in his breath then tugged hard. The fork came free, tearing the kid's shirtsleeve and the pinioned muscle beneath. Blood spurted from the angry wound. The cowboy winced with the sudden jolt of agony, but managed to retain his dignity.

'We need to get you to a sawbones,' Gleeson said, untying the kid's necker and wrapping it around the injury.

'I ain't the only one who needs treating,' Jones observed, indicating the bloody bandage around his partner's head.

The remark fleetingly helped to lighten the grim incident. Then Gleeson suddenly remembered that Vandyke was still at large. He backed off, hunkering down while scanning the immediate vicinity. The revolver panned across the corral. But there was no sign of the outlaw chieftain.

So where was he?

Then it hit him between the eyes like a fireball from Hell.

The varmint had always carried a torch for Lucy. Seeing that the battle had gone against him, he must have decided to cut his losses, and once again take the woman hostage.

'You OK to rest up here for a spell?' Gleeson

enquired of his partner. 'Dutch Henry still has to be dealt with.'

Not waiting for an answer, he hurried out of the barn and headed for his store. On the off-chance that the Dutchman was lying in wait, he took a back route behind the buildings fronting Main Street.

On reaching the back of the store, his supposition regarding the outlaw's logic proved to be correct. The skunk had just emerged through the rear door. An arm was draped around Lucy's neck with his hand firmly clamped over her mouth to prevent any cries for help. The other one held a gun to her head.

'Stay right where you are, Dutch.' The directive was blunt and unequivocal. 'You harm one hair of her head and you're a dead man.'

'I'm a goner anyway thanks to you,' Vandyke snarled. Vehement rancour at having once again been bested showed on the twisted visage. 'But at least I can get away whilst I have the woman. Step aside or she gets it.' He racked back the hammer to stress his grave intent. 'Now drop that gun.'

Gleeson had no doubts that the reckless killer would carry out his threat if pushed too far. He held up his hands in surrender, but still kept hold of the revolver. One final declaration was made to buy time.

'Don't think for a moment that I won't track you down.'

The venomous pledge of retribution received a scornful guffaw. 'You'll have to catch me first.' A murderous glint showed in the killer's narrowed gaze. 'And I sure ain't gonna allow that to happen.' His gun shifted towards the ex-lawman. Then he hesitated. 'One thing has been puzzling me about you, Gleeson.'

The ex-lawman waited.

'Most starpackers are doing a job when they go after guys like me. But you made it personal.'

'Remember that lawman you gunned down in Wichita?' Gleeson fixed the killer with a feral eye. 'Well, he was my brother.'

Vandyke's face registered surprise and understanding in equal measure. The declaration had distracted him sufficiently to give Lucy the chance to turn the tables on the outlaw.

It would be her only opportunity to prevent her husband being shot down.

She managed to open her mouth and bite down hard on to the hand covering her mouth. The sudden jolt of pain caused the killer to slacken his grip. The pregnant woman was then able to wriggle out of his clutches.

That was all the incentive Chad Gleeson needed. His hand dropped like a stone, the Colt Frontier barking angrily. Two bullets perfectly placed finished Dutch Henry's resurrected outlaw career. Lucy swayed. The trauma of yet another potential kidnapping was almost too much to bear in her condition.

Gleeson quickly stepped forward before she fainted away. He held her close for five long minutes. A comforting silence descended over the battleground. It was finally broken when young Squirrel-Tooth Jones appeared.

'I heard the shots,' he said. 'Figured you might need

some more help.'

Gleeson offered him a wan smile. 'All in hand, old buddy, all in hand.'

Doors along the main street slowly opened as the good citizens of Casa Grande emerged from their holes. The three principals of the conflict ignored them as they slowly walked up Main Street and entered the general store.

There was much to think on regarding their future in Casa Grande. The town had let them down. And for that kind of betrayal, Seven-Up Chad Gleeson was reluctant to offer any forgiveness.

Maybe it was time to move on.

Staffordshire Library and Information Services
Please return or renew by the last date shown

If not required by other readers, this item may be renewed in
person, by post or telephone, online or by email.
To renew, either the book or ticket are required.

24 Hour Renewal Line
0845 33 00 740

Staffordshire
County Council

Staffordshire

3 8014 11034 1010